Leaving Jetty Road

rebecca burton

Published by Laurel-Leaf
an imprint of Random House Children's Books
a division of Random House, Inc.
New York

Originally published in hardcover in the United States by Alfred A. Knopf Books for Young Readers, New York, in 2006. This edition published by arrangement with Alfred A. Knopf Books for Young Readers.

www.randomhouse.com/teens

Educators and librarians, for a variety of teaching tools, visit us at
www.randomhouse.com/teachers

RL: 5.8
ISBN: 978-0-553-49505-8
March 2008
Printed in the United States of America
10 9 8 7 6 5 4 3 2
First Laurel-Leaf Edition

To Glenn, Grace, Robbi, and Sylvia,
my four writer friends:
because you listened so hard,
and write so well

prologue

Nat

There are two kinds of people in life: the swimmers and the drifters.

It's like, some people swim purposefully through their lives, always knowing where they're headed, always looking strong and fit and ready to get there. Others, well, they don't sink, and they don't swim; they just *drift*. You know?

It's easy to tell who's a swimmer and who's a drifter. Take Lise and Sofia and me, for example, on a hot Sunday afternoon toward the end of December. We're sitting on the carpet in my parents' living room, the three of us, arguing in lazy, sweaty voices about what movie we're going to see in town this evening. But it's too hot to go anywhere; at 100 degrees, it's too hot to do *anything* except sit and talk.

"You thought about New Year's resolutions yet?" Lise asks suddenly.

Sofia and I look over at her.

"No, seriously," she says, gazing steadily back at us. "Next year's Year *12*. You've *got* to make a resolution."

New Year's resolutions are Lise's "thing." Every year, she makes one. She thinks about it carefully, writes it down on a big sheet of paper, and pins the paper up over the desk in her bedroom. Usually, it's something fairly everyday, like *Study harder,* or *Practice the piano every night.* In Year 11, though, she made a resolution that she'd never drink alcohol again. Not that she ever drank much to begin with, but "it's bad for you," she said simply. "It's *addictive.*"

Most people break their New Year's resolutions, right? But not Lise. She hasn't had a drop to drink since.

"Anyway," she announces now, without warning. "This year I've decided to go vegetarian." She glances at us, sees the expressions on our faces, says hastily, "Not forever, okay? Just to see what it's like."

Then, before either of us can say anything, she gets up and goes over to her bag, propped against the wall in the corner of the room. She pulls a video out of it and holds it up to us triumphantly. *Cruelty to Animals,* says the title on the cover.

Sofia groans. "Where did you get *that* from?"

"Just let me put it on, okay?" says Lise. "If you don't like it, we can always switch it off."

We sprawl out on our stomachs on the floor to watch the video, with the ceiling fans whirring madly to stir up the hot, still air and my brother Tim's latest heavy metal CD reverberating through the walls. At the start we're still chattering away, but by the end we're sitting there in total silence, our faces riveted to the screen. *Cruelty to Animals.* It's the kind of video you know you'll never forget. I knew about slaughterhouses and animal experimentation in theory—but it's different when you see it in the flesh.

"So how about it?" says Lise afterward. "Going vegetarian, I mean." She pauses, pushes the heavy mop of hair back from her face. "Just for a year. That's all. Just to see if we can do it."

I mean, what can we say? I can't get the picture of those slaughterhouses out of my head.

So we shake hands on it.

"No more barbecues," says Sofia wistfully.

I sigh. "I can't imagine a whole year without sausages and tomato sauce."

"Or chops."

"Or roast lamb."

"Or gyros!"

But Lise just smiles. "Vegetarianism's good for you, you know. Think of all the *weight* we could lose."

That's the thing about Lise: she's so *determined*. She's quiet, shy; solitary, even—but when she sets herself a goal, she goes out and achieves it, no matter what it takes. That's what I mean about swimmers and drifters: she's a swimmer through and through.

So's Sofia—in a completely different way. She isn't focused like Lise; she's more of a happy-go-lucky, anything-goes kind of person. At school she carries around a pack of cigarettes in her bag, like she's some kind of rebel or something; and sometimes, before Assembly, you'll find her under the peppercorn trees at the back of the tennis courts, puffing madly away. But then get her on the subject of her younger half brother, Mattie, and she's as sweet and domesticated as they come. She even cooks dinner every night when she comes home after school, just to make sure he gets a "nourishing meal." ("Mate, Mum's *hopeless.* If I didn't cook, we'd live on pizza and baked beans every night of the week.")

She follows nobody's rules but her own, Sofe. That's what makes her a swimmer. She just strikes out in her own direction and never looks back.

Me? I'm the ultimate drifter. *Tinker, tailor, soldier, sailor . . .* I've never known where I'm going, what I want to do with my life. What I want to *be.* Next year Lise is gearing up for trying to get into law (which she'll sail into), and Sofe has vague plans for nursing (because it's a good job for traveling). Me, I still don't even know if I want to go to university. Decision making is hard work: even *thinking* about it's hard work.

Sometimes I feel like I'm so unmotivated, you know? So boring. It's like I'm just *floating through life.*

Beside me, Lise rolls onto her stomach, her feet kicking the air. She has this pale, pale skin, Lise: it gets even paler on hot days, and dark smudges form under her eyes where the sweat collects. Somehow it makes her face look even more intense than usual. Right now, looking at her, I find myself thinking about what she said earlier: *Next year's Year 12. You've GOT to make a resolution.*

The thing is, there are heaps of resolutions I could make.

I could study hard right from the start of the year instead of leaving it to the last moment, like I usually do. I could get that weekend job I've been talking about for so long; start saving up, at last, for a car. I could learn how to cook something other than chocolate cake—I mean, who else is going to cook all those vegetarian meals I have ahead of me? My mother's a *lousy* cook.

Or you know what? I could just—stop drifting.

PART I

Nat

chapter one

The beach

I've been fighting with my brother Tim about who gets to drive the Mini ever since I got my P-plates last year.

"Just because you got your licence before me doesn't mean it's your car, Tim. Mum and Dad gave it to us to *share.*"

"You're still a bloody P-plater. You'd crash it the first time you took it out."

"At least I don't drive when I'm *drunk.*"

This is a sore point with Tim. A few months ago, he drove over to a party—the eighteenth birthday for one of his mates from the building site where he works. He left the party around midnight, drove home at just under the speed limit, took the side streets all the way. He got in at half past twelve, crowing over having dodged the police and ready for a few million liters of water before bed. ("Best way to get over a hangover, Nat. You just remember that.")

But there, looking up at him from the old floral couch in

the living room, were Mum and Dad. Just sitting there, waiting for him.

"I can smell your breath a mile away," Dad said wryly, and took the car keys away from him for four weeks.

But that was months ago. Since then, Tim's guarded those keys even more jealously than before.

So *that's* why I've got to get a job.

One day a few weeks after New Year's, I mention this to Lise. We're at the beach, lying on our towels on the sand, sunscreen plastered across our faces, legs kicking the air. It's hot, and Lise is looking kind of—not bored at my conversation, exactly, but not overly thrilled, either. I guess it's only about the millionth time I've talked about it to her.

"But I mean, *think* about it," I say, trying to make my point. "If I got a job, this time next year I could have my *own* car."

This beach trip: it's a regular Lise-and-me thing. We do it every summer on the last Saturday before the new school year begins. The first time was at the end of Year 7, which was the year Lise and I met, the year we became best friends. Mum took us that day. She packed a picnic lunch—squashed Vegemite sandwiches and juice boxes, and red Popsicles that melted in the cooler on the tram. Then she lay on the beach and read her book while Lise and I swam and threw the Frisbee at each other, and compared bathing suits and beach towels. We've come back by ourselves every year since, meeting at the tram stop near Lise's house. We always go to the same beach, at the end of Jetty Road: Glenelg—my favorite stretch of sea in Adelaide, my favorite summer place.

Today, like every other year, we've spent the time swimming and snoozing, lying under the jetty between swims, staring up at the wooden beams and talking. When I say talking, I mean, like—*talking.* Hopes and dreams; plans and fears; life, the universe, and everything—you name it, Lise and I'll talk about it. You know what I mean?

But now, when I've finally talked myself out about getting a job, she goes all funny on me.

"It's Year *12,* Nat."

"So?"

"Well, aren't we meant to be studying or something? I *have* to get into law."

"Lise—" I sigh. She's been saying she wants to do law ever since I met her. "You'll get into law with your eyes closed."

She pulls a face. "Maybe."

"Anyway, I only meant a one-day-a-week kind of job. You've got to have *some* kind of break from studying."

She shrugs, and doesn't answer. Then she goes kind of quiet.

When Lise is annoyed, she lets her hair (which is thick and curly and, at the moment, very damp) fall in front of her face, so you can't see what she's thinking. That stuff I said before, about talking? The one thing she and I don't ever talk about is what makes Lise angry, and why. But you sure as hell know *when* she's angry. The silent treatment: that's what she gives you. ("The sulk" is what Sofia calls it.)

One thing's for sure: she's giving it to me now. I glance across at her, elbow propping my chin, wondering what I've said. She ignores me and stares at the sand, tracing patterns in it with the sharp edge of a broken shell, her face completely obscured by her hair.

Clearly, there is no point going on with this conversation.

I sigh, give up talking, roll over onto my back. In my head, lying next to Lise, I go on dreaming about having a job, a car, money. I mean, there's no harm dreaming, surely?

Sand prickles my shoulder blades, and the towel creases damply, stickily, beneath my back. The sky throbs above us, late-January blue.

Afterward, we walk back up Jetty Road toward the tram, soggy bathing suits scrumpled up in our bags. Waves of heat swell up from the pavement toward us, and the asphalt pulses under our feet. I straggle along beside Lise, dreaming of ice cream, and cold drinks, and air-conditioning. Already it feels like we never went swimming at all.

But it's weird, sometimes, how things you really, really want can suddenly just *appear,* right there in front of you. My mother's got this summed up in three words: "Life is good." (That's Mum for you—ever the social worker, ever the optimist. She's *determined* to implant positive thoughts into her kids' minds.) Sofia just calls it fate. "If it's meant to happen, it'll happen, Nat," she's always telling me. As in, *Just go with the flow.*

Anyway, whatever—something I've been wanting for *ages* happens now, just as we're crossing at the traffic lights about halfway down the road.

Lise reaches the other side of the road before I do. (She always walks so quickly, Lise—like she's in a real hurry to get somewhere.) But then, instead of going on farther up the road, she stops suddenly. It's not that she's waiting for me: she's standing, staring through the window of the little health food café on the corner. It looks like she's seen something she hadn't expected to see.

"What?" I say, catching up with her.

"Look." She points at a piece of paper pinned up in the café's window.

In dark blue pen, the writing on the piece of paper says:

Kitchen hand / waitress needed.
Saturdays only, no experience necessary.
Interest in health foods required.

"Hey!" I say excitedly. "D'you think being vegetarian counts as having an 'interest in health foods'?"

Lise pushes a coil of long brown hair back over her shoulder. "I s'pose—"

"You could apply, too, you know. They'd probably interview us right now. We could just go in and ask."

"Nat." Lise is looking at me like I'm crazy. "You're not serious."

The metal tram tracks lining the street glint up at me, hot and black. Sweat trickles down my nose; my T-shirt sticks to my chest. The skin on my arms feels parched, burning, after the cool salt of the sea.

"Why not?" I say. "At least it'll be cooler in there. And think of all the movies you could afford to go to if you're the one who gets the job."

Lise is the only person I know who likes movies more than I do; she's the biggest movie freak this side of the Nullarbor Plain. I knew that would suck her in.

I push open the coffee shop door before either of us can change my mind.

Afterward, to pacify Lise, we wander over to the Italian café opposite the cinema, a little farther up the street.

"Gelato? Or coffee?"

"Coffee," says Lise instantly. *"Cappuccino."* It's her favorite drink.

We sit at a table by the wall, away from the glare of the big glass windows that front the street, soaking up the air-conditioning. Opposite me, dreamy with coolness, Lise spoons up her froth. I can smell the salt in my hair; my skin is white-crusted with it.

"If there was one thing—just *one* thing—you could change about yourself," Lise says suddenly, "what would it be?"

She does this heaps, Lise: asks you these deep, intense questions right out of the blue. Like that's what you've been talking about all along.

"Lots of stuff," I say, without giving it too much thought. "I'd argue with Tim less. I wouldn't lose my temper so much." I grin at her: "And I'd spend less money on cappuccinos."

"They're all *little* things," she objects. "I mean the *big* stuff."

I think seriously this time. "I'd like to be more decisive, you know? I'd like to work out what I actually want to *do* with my life."

There it is again—this drifting thing of mine. I wish I could describe properly how it feels. It's not unhappiness—not at all. I mean, I'm the kind of person who gets high on going out for coffee, or having a night at the movies. It's not laziness, exactly, either. What I'm talking about is more a kind of indecisiveness, of *not knowing,* even about the stupidest things. You know, like—which TV program to watch, or how many books to borrow from the library. I can't even decide what kind of music to listen to, because I change my mind about what I like all the time. (Once or twice, I've even found myself humming along quite happily to my dad's country-and-western albums. Now *that's* a worry.)

I'm like this with guys, too. I don't have a boyfriend—never have. I've had a few crushes, of course, and there have even been one or two guys who were drunk enough to make a pass at me. (Unlike Lise, whose only male experience so far has been my brother Tim's constant teasing over the years.) But basically, I just can't make up my mind what kind of guy I like. Or what kind of guy might actually like me.

My mother's solution to this kind of thing is to do a course. You know, like—a workshop. "Get to *know* yourself, sweetie," she's always saying to me.

Mum thinks that talking is the solution to everything. Maybe it's because she's a social worker: I reckon her biggest nightmare would be if she thought that either Tim or I had some problem and we were worrying about it by ourselves. You know, like—*alone.* Not *saying* anything to anyone.

In fact, that's the way she and Dad have tried to bring us up to deal with everything: to "talk things through." Our family doesn't have "arguments"; we practice what Mum calls "conflict resolution." We don't yell and scream at each other; we have "roundtable discussions." When we were little, Tim and I used to spend hours trying to work out why they were called that when the only table we ever sat around was the kitchen one, which is rectangular.

But the upbringing kind of misfired on me, I think. Now I just try and avoid confrontation altogether, especially with my family. Just the thought of all that self-analysis makes me shudder. I don't want to talk about stuff, to think about it. I just want to *do* it. I want to *try* it, and see what happens. How else am I going to find out about life? How else am I going to *decide*?

"What about you?" I ask Lise now. "What would *you* change about yourself?"

She doesn't answer. For ages, she doesn't answer. She picks up an unopened sugar packet from the table, creases it into tiny, deliberate folds, then unfolds it again, smoothing the wrinkles out of the paper. She frowns. Then she says quietly, "I'd change everything."

"Everything?" I echo.

She nods, looking down. "My clothes. My body. My *self.* I'd like to get outside of myself and be someone else completely."

This is something else Lise does a lot; she says this stuff—this negative stuff—about herself. I mean, what are you supposed to *say* when someone says something like that?

So I do what I always do (what Mum would *never* do): I change the subject.

"How about another cappuccino?" I suggest lightly. I grab my purse, stand up. "Or a bowl of gelato? We could share one."

Immediately her face brightens up.

"Yes, please." She hands me some money. "Life's got to be all right if there's a cappuccino on the way, right?"

"Exactly," I say, and head for the counter.

She doesn't bring the subject up again when I come back, and for the rest of the afternoon we talk about other things—you know, much more important things, like what movie we'll go to see next weekend and what color Lucy Davison will have dyed her hair for the first day of term (it's a different color every year, without fail) and who our biology teacher will be this year.

"I can't *believe* Mr. Schumacher got sacked last year," Lise says. "He was a great biology teacher."

"Sofe says it was for 'getting involved' with one of the Year 12 students."

She wrinkles her forehead. "Like—what does that mean exactly, 'getting involved'?"

Our eyes dance wickedly as we look at each other across the table.

"You think he felt her up?"

"Or kissed her?"

"Maybe they had sex in the lab assistant's room."

"Yeah—on the desk. Next to that jar with the pickled brain in it."

I could have asked Lise what she really *meant* about wanting to change all those things about herself, I suppose. But to be honest, I didn't want to know.

I still don't, either. Everyone wants to change *something* about themselves, you know? What's the point of getting hung up about it? Sometimes you just have to move on from that stuff, think about something else. That's *my* theory, anyway. I think Lise just needs to be reminded of that every now and then.

That's my *other* theory: maybe if I remind her often enough, she'll remember it for herself one of these days. I mean, if I can get myself to do the reminding, surely she can start putting it into practice.

Maybe.

chapter two

The Wild Carrot Café

If it's meant to happen, it'll happen. On the first day of term, I break my news to Lise and Sofe.

"He rang me up on Sunday to tell me I got the job."

Sofe gives me a quick, pleased grin. "You mean the guy at the café in Glenelg who interviewed you both?"

I nod. "Yeah. The manager." I turn cautiously to Lise, not sure what her reaction will be. "You remember—Michael?"

But Lise just shrugs. "I didn't want to work there anyway. There's too much studying this year."

Probably she's upset. Not because she really wanted to work at the café—I believe her when she says she didn't—but because I got the job and she didn't. As in, *Nat's better than me*—that kind of thing.

But I think the truth of it is, I just talked to Michael more than she did. Lise, being shy, hardly said anything at all.

When I say Lise is shy, I mean, like—*shy.* Put her with people she doesn't know very well and she goes sort of quiet and stiff, like she's got nothing to say. It's even worse when she's with guys. Even Tim, whom she's known for years: when he's around, she's this completely different person; you can't get a word out of her. It's like she shuts in on herself. Her face gets all *boxed in.* Only her lovely wild hair seems free.

I don't get it, to be honest. I mean, last year I had this crush on one of Tim's mates from work, Mario. It was huge: I used to lie in bed at night for hours, just thinking about him. He stayed over at our house for dinner a couple of nights, and the whole time, all I wanted to do was reach out and *touch* him. Just feel *close* to him, you know? Of course I never said anything to him about it. How could I? He was my brother's friend; you can't get more embarrassing than that.

So yes, in one way, because of all that, I felt pretty shy around him. But it never made me so shy I couldn't speak. Besides, the thing is, you get over those feelings, and you move on. You know?

But Lise hasn't moved on—not at all. If anything, her shyness seems to have gotten worse as she's gotten older. Sometimes I think she'll never change.

On my first day at the Wild Carrot Café, it's 100 degrees.

Michael, the manager, is apologetic. "I've got the ceiling fans on high. Doesn't seem to make much of a difference, though." He runs a stubby hand through his short gray hair. "One of these days we'll get air-conditioning."

He shows me around the place again, more slowly than he did during the interview. There are wooden floorboards all the way through to the kitchen, scrubbed to a dull, worn gleam. A small black tub of wheatgrass decorates each of the tables, which are covered with unbleached tablecloths and burlap place mats. ("Very unfashionable to have tablecloths these days, I know," says Michael, bustling around, tugging at a cloth to straighten it, pushing a sugar pot back into the center of the table. "Butcher paper's all the rage. But I can't stand the stuff. It's so unrestful.")

Potted plants in terra-cotta-colored containers line the walls, and rough wooden crates filled with apples and oranges stand in each corner of the shop. More tubs of wheatgrass stand at each end of the counter. It's got what you call the natural look. Almost—but not quite—twee.

Michael introduces me to a girl with dark, curly hair and a wart on her upper lip who's standing at the espresso machine behind the counter, wrapping knives and forks up in paper napkins.

"Loretta's a uni student. She works here on Saturdays and Sundays. She starts at ten, an hour before you."

Loretta glances up at me with a lazy, hungover smile.

"That's on the days when she *makes* it here, of course," says Michael grimly, and hurries me on out the back to the kitchen.

"And this is our chef, Joshua."

Joshua's standing at the counter opposite the dishwasher, chopping veggies. He turns around and smiles at me in greeting.

And that's it. There's no warning. One minute I'm feeling normal (if a bit nervous about whether I'm actually going to *like* it, working here); the next minute Joshua the chef is smiling at me—and my knees are crumbling.

He's like—gorgeous. *Drop-dead.*

He has brown-brown eyes, an Asian-style brocaded cloth cap in place of the usual chef's hat, and a swoop of blond hair that falls over his forehead. He's tall, tall, tall, and his black-and-white checked chef's pants seem to go on for miles.

"Hope you like wheatgrass," he says, grinning.

"Me? I practically *inhale* the stuff," I answer, like my legs aren't trembling and my cheeks aren't beet-red.

His eyes dance at me. "You've come to the right place, then."

Next to me, Michael glances at his watch.

"There's just time to teach you how to make cappuccinos before the lunchtime rush, Natalie. I'll get Loretta to show you."

He pushes back through the wooden swinging doors to the front of the shop, a small, sturdy, middle-aged man, always hurrying, always on the run. He's going to be a hard taskmaster; I can tell that already. I follow him out, but not before Josh gives me another one of those smiles and my knees turn to complete sawdust.

Everything has changed. Just like that. All day, I can't stop smiling; and when Michael compliments me on my great "people skills," I feel almost guilty. It's not exactly the *work* that's making me so friendly to all the customers.

But I'm sure I can muster up enough enthusiasm to keep Michael happy, as long as Joshua keeps working at the café.

chapter three

House in the hills

"Only one more year of singing hymns and saying the Lord's Prayer," says Sofia to me on Monday morning as we line up outside the school hall for Assembly. She pushes her ponytail impatiently back behind her shoulder. "I should do what Lise does, hey. Join all the school clubs in sight. What's she at this morning—chess club? Math club? Or was it choir?"

"I don't think she goes to all those clubs just to get out of Assembly," I say mildly. "She does actually want to be in them."

"That has to be the saddest thing I've heard this morning," Sofia says darkly.

I'm just about to protest (I can't *stand* the way Sofe makes comments like this about Lise) when she goes on, dreamily, "Anyway, just think—this time next year I won't even *remember* the words to the Lord's Prayer."

She grumbles at me all the time about going to an all-girls

school, Sofia. Before she came here at the beginning of Year 11, she went to some kind of "alternative" school in the hills, near where she and her little half brother and her mum live. She's always going on to Lise and me about how much more fun it was at her old school. Didn't matter whether you wore track pants or Calvin Klein, she says; the guys'd still crack farts in the locker room, and the girls scored highest on all the chemistry tests.

Sometimes, when she says this, Lise nods worriedly. "I'm sure it's not *normal* spending all your time with girls."

It's one of the few things Sofe and Lise ever actually agree on. Sometimes I wish—you have no *idea* how much I wish—there were more of those things.

Me, I like our school. I like the teachers, the subjects; I even like the uniform. (Well, it's not that I *like* the uniform, exactly; what I like is not having to decide what you're going to wear to school every morning.) On hot days the classrooms are drenched with the smell of crushed, seed-spilling fruit rotting underneath the old Moreton Bay fig tree in the schoolyard. At recess, I stand peeling oranges with Lise and Sofia under this tree, and we trace our feet along the thick roots that crack through the asphalt in wide, solid rivulets. I feel *comfortable* here.

After Assembly, Sofia and I walk across the schoolyard toward the Year 12 locker room.

"Hey, guess what?" she says. "I got invited to a party."

I wait patiently while she kneels at her locker, sorting through her books. "Who by?"

"A guy at the Aquatic Centre. He was sitting next to me in the spa."

"Sofe," I groan.

"Mate, he was *nice.*" She looks up at me with that big, wide smile of hers (a flash of white teeth in an olive-brown face; it's a smile that all the guys fall for). "He goes to uni."

"What—studying how to chat up cute little schoolgirls in the swimming pool?"

Things like this are always happening to Sofia. It's funny, really: I mean, she's tall, blond-haired, and blue-eyed, but there's a big bump in the middle of her nose, and her hair is thin and always has split ends. Still, the guys practically swarm around her. She, of course, takes it all for granted. "They're just guys, Nat," she said to me once, dismissively. "It's just *sex.*"

Now she stands up, her arms full of books and loose-leaf folders.

"His name's Nick," she offers. "Hey, and guess what? He's vegetarian, too."

We trudge upstairs for English. Outside the classroom, we lean against the wooden rails of the balcony, books and folders piled up by our feet, waiting with the rest of the class for Mr. Adams to come and unlock the door. Sofia falls uncharacteristically silent, twisting her ponytail around and around one finger, eyes far away, nose wrinkled in thought. The sound of a gym teacher's whistle drifts up to us from the Oval.

"So are you going?" I ask at last.

"Where?"

"To the party. On Saturday."

She looks at me like I'm stupid. "Of *course.*"

"Sofia Walker," I say, giving up.

She gathers her books back up in her arms as Mr. Adams approaches, keys jangling from his belt. "Give me a ring on Sunday and I'll tell you what happened, okay?" Then she grins mischievously. "Let me know if you want the censored version or the uncensored."

With Sofia, the censored version is always the safest option. In any case, she'll break up with him soon. I give her three weeks, max.

A couple of weeks later, I go up to her house after work on Saturday, to stay the night.

I love going to visit Sofia. Partly, I think, it's just because I hardly ever get to do it: she lives in the hills, which means that from school, you have to catch a bus into town and then a train back out again to get there. Even the house itself is another ten-minute walk from the train station, with a steep and windy driveway at the end of it. I always arrive there red-cheeked and gasping for breath.

Because of that, even if I'd known her as long as I've known Lise, I probably still wouldn't see as much of her outside of school. Lise and I live just a few streets away from each other—she's one tram stop closer to the city than me—and we're always in and out of each other's houses. When we were younger, it was like we lived in each other's pockets.

But the other reason I like staying at Sofe's is that her life is so *different* from mine and Lise's. Her father, for example, left years ago. One day, when Sofe was just a toddler, her mother went out to the supermarket to get some milk, and when she came back, he'd just *gone.* He didn't even take his clothes with him.

Sofia's mother runs a jam-making business from home, and she told me all this the first time I visited. She was standing at the stove, stirring something in a big pot.

"It was like he wanted to pretend he'd never lived there at all," she said in this hurt, wondering kind of voice.

Sofe rolled her eyes and said impatiently, *"Mum."* Then she turned to me. "Mum's been *dying* for a new female audience. I don't think I've brought a girlfriend up here since *primary* school."

At the time, I wondered how that could possibly be true. I mean, you'd expect, with a mother who thinks men are positively *evil,* that Sofe might have grown up the same way, you know? ("You haven't heard the story about my stepdad, Nat," she said to me later that day. "You just wait till she tells you that one.") But now I know it's the truth. Sofe just hasn't hung around girls much over the last few years: "I like guys. I like the way they think"—a flash of that wicked smile—"and I like the way they *look.*"

That reminds me of something else about Sofe. Her mum is what you might call "permissive"—she's got a dope plant growing in the backyard, and she's quite happy for Sofe to bring her boyfriends home for the night. "At least that way I know where she is," she once told me solemnly. "And plus—I get to meet the boyfriend the next morning."

This Saturday, by the time her mother picks me up at the station it's almost dusk. Before dinner—which is pizza, because Sofe's on strike ("I'm sick of cooking all the time") and her mother's too busy labeling jam jars for a greenmarket the following morning—we sit on the brightly colored rug in Sofia's bedroom, gossiping. She shows me some clothes she bought at a thrift store, gets me to try on a pair of her earrings.

"So how's work going?" she asks me eventually.

I grimace. "I *hate* washing dishes. And I'm crap at making cappuccinos. But I still think the chef's pretty cute."

"What did you say his name was again?"

I try to say his name without blushing, but I can't. "Joshua."

She gives me a cheeky look. "You should ask him out."

"*Sofe.* No *way*! He's at least nineteen."

She smiles deviously. "I've always thought you'd go for older men in uniform."

When the pizza arrives—vegetarian, of course!—we go and sit on the porch in the backyard, with Sofe's mum and her little half brother, Mattie. (I have by now, of course, heard the famous story involving Mattie's father. He left for India when Sofia was ten and Mattie was three, to get "enlightened." They never heard from him again: "He got so enlightened, he just *forgot* about paying child support" is the way Sofia's mother puts it.) After we've finished eating, we stay outside for a while, and Mattie pesters us (unsuccessfully) to play cricket with him. Sofe pulls out a pack of cigarettes, and she and her mother light up. I sip my orange juice.

"Nick coming up at all this weekend?" Sofia's mother asks.

Sofe shrugs. "Maybe. Not for the night."

"Not going *swimming* with him, Sofe?" I needle her.

She lets out a puff of smoke into the night. "What d'you mean?"

"Well, he *did* pick you up at the Aquatic Centre."

She groans. "Get over it, Nat. There are worse places to meet a guy."

The truth is, I can't really explain why I feel so happy when I'm at Sofe's house. It could be all sorts of things—the view over the hills from the front garden, the smell of jam cooking on the stove, Mattie's wide, happy smile. The arguments Sofe and her mum have: short, sharp, simple (*totally* unlike the arguments I have with *my* mother, which are few but somehow always fraught with resentment). Or it could just be the way school seems so far away.

Sometimes, though, I think it's just because Sofe is *there*—because she's a second friend, an alternative to Lise. That sounds weird, but what I mean is, I've always enjoyed meeting new people. At primary school, I had this series of short, intense friendships: In Year 3, Eleni Stavros was my best friend; in Year 4, it was Paul Hastings. In Year 6, for a few months, I hung around with Mandy Martin, who made me giggle and was always getting into trouble with the teachers, and who eventually, to my half-admiring dismay, got expelled. (No one ever knew why: she wouldn't even tell *me;* and then her family just moved away.)

It was the same with Lise and me, to begin with: I guess she was just my next new friend—only, unlike the others before her, she stuck around. I like that about Lise: her loyalty; the way she grows *with* you, instead of *away* from you. I just wish she was also more interested in other people: I wish she liked meeting them, wish she wanted to get to know them. Sofia, like me, does.

Maybe, in the end, that's what I like about going up to her house. I like the difference, the change of pace. I like the contrast. I like the *change.*

chapter four

Broccoli dreams

"I'm going to ride to Perth next year," Josh tells me the next Saturday at the Wild Carrot.

I look up at him from the sink. "You got a motorbike?"

"Nah. I'm going on my bicycle."

I stare at him incredulously. "But *why*?"

"Why not?" he says, laughing at my astonishment.

It's half past three and we're alone in the kitchen. The café is deserted (the "midafternoon lull," Michael calls it), and Loretta's sitting at one of the tables near the window, on her lunch break. Michael, having sent me into the kitchen to catch up on the dirty dishes, is standing outside, talking to one of the "regulars" on the pavement.

This is the first day I've spent any time alone with Josh at all since I started working at the café a few weeks ago. To my surprise, we haven't stopped talking since the moment I got in here at the end of the lunchtime rush.

"I finish my apprenticeship at the end of this year," he says now, taking a ball of scone dough out of the Kenwood mixer and flattening it slightly on the chopping board. "I thought a bike trip would be a good way to celebrate. I rode to Sydney the year I left high school, and ever since then I've been wanting to try Perth."

"That's your idea of a celebration?"

He has this way of looking at you while you talk, Josh—head tilted to the side, one eyebrow raised. I've noticed it before as I was running in from the counter to give him another order: it makes my stomach tremble. Now I turn away from him quickly, slide another rack of dirty plates into the dishwasher.

"You just want to die of dehydration and muscle meltdown out in the desert. That's what it is, really—hey, Josh?"

He grins as he pushes the scone cutter into the dough, and the smile breaks up the wrinkle of intense concentration on his forehead.

"How *did* you guess? 'Young chef dies in tragic cycling accident 200 miles west of Ceduna.' What d'you reckon?"

What I reckon is, his dark brown eyes are just the color of chocolate, and the way he looks down at me from behind those thick blond bangs is driving me crazy. He's so fit, so motivated, so gorgeous, so . . . all of the things I'm not. The real tragedy, if you ask me, is that he's somehow got it into his head that it's worth wasting time talking to me.

"I'd rather bake a cake," I say quickly. "Or curl up with a book for a few days." I'm trying to let him know, before it's too late, that I am definitely not interesting; I am *definitely* not his type.

He bends down, opens the oven door, shoves in a batch of dough. "What kind of cake?"

"Chocolate cake. It's the only thing I can cook," I explain, just to make it completely obvious how uninteresting and untalented I am.

But he smiles at me, one eyebrow raised again. "With icing, right?"

"Of course," I say helplessly. "The icing's the best bit."

I turn hastily back to the sink, start scrubbing away at the latest dirty pan. (If only you could put *that* through the dishwasher!) Behind me, I hear heavy, booted footsteps: Josh, coming toward me from the other side of the kitchen. He stops just behind me as I reach out for the hot water tap; he is so close that I can feel his breath, warm and even, on my neck. I stand still, taut, just *waiting*. Then—slowly, deliberately—he reaches out, puts his hand over mine on the tap.

"Shouldn't wash dishes under a running tap, Nat," he says softly. "It wastes water."

His fingers guide mine, switching the tap off. Then he stands there, looking down at me. Not moving away. Not letting go of my hand.

I will *melt*. I am *convinced* I will melt.

After work, instead of heading toward the nearest tram stop, which is just up the road, I wander down Jetty Road toward the terminus, by the beachfront. I'm not ready for home yet. There are too many good things to think about from this afternoon; and, besides, if I can't wipe the stupid, happy grin off my face, Tim will be merciless all evening.

I walk past the terminus outside the hotel on the esplanade, across the brick-paved plaza and the beachfront lawns. There's a low stone wall that fences the esplanade in from the beach, and I go and sit on it, feet dangling over the other side. Music from the hotel drifts toward me, loud, pumping, insistent. People wander past toward the jetty, licking ice cream—an old lady talking to a younger woman, probably her daughter, who is pushing a stroller; a skinny man with dreadlocks, tugged along by his scruffy-looking dog; a neatly dressed couple, each holding one hand of a fat, short-haired little kid with Down's syndrome. The sea lies pearl-blue, like satin under the pink sky, and three pelicans glide above the water, in formation.

"Hey—*Nat*!"

I turn around. It's Josh, striding toward me past Fasta Pasta and the hotel, waving.

"So I'm not the only one who goes to the beach after work," he says, dropping his voice as he comes closer.

"I wanted to see the sun set first, before the tram gets here."

He cocks his head at me. "No driver's license yet?"

"I've got the *license.* My brother just won't let me use the *car.*"

"Oh, well," he says. "Catching the tram saves fuel, anyway, right? Which is always a good thing."

Oh, *hell.* Not only is the guy fit, gorgeous, and motivated—he's also a *greenie.* Now I know I have absolutely *no* chance with him at all.

"Anyway, it's lucky I saw you here." He sits down on the

wall beside me, swings his legs over as he hands me something in one of the takeaway containers from the café. "I've got some leftovers, from lunch. I noticed you didn't have much of a break—unlike Loretta."

I lift one corner of the lid, smell the contents. "Mmm—yum. *Broccoli.*"

He looks at me, amused. "You like broccoli?"

"It's not like I'm a health freak or anything," I say hastily. "It's just, ever since I went vegetarian, I've had these huge cravings for broccoli. It's really weird. I even *dream* about broccoli sometimes."

Josh kicks his heels against the wall, his long legs dangling. "Broccoli dreams . . . ," he says musingly.

I take a bite, feeling his eyes on me.

"This is *delicious.* It's a stir-fry, right?" He nods. "D'you have any other broccoli recipes, by any chance?"

"How does broccoli pesto sound?"

He loves cooking, Josh; you can see it from the way he works at the Wild Carrot. Me, I get sick of frothing milk for all those cappuccinos. (It's especially hard on hot days; apparently it's to do with the lack of protein in the dry summer grass or something. When there's less protein in the grass that the cows eat, the milk doesn't froth: it just stays flat.) Michael, meanwhile, buzzes around impatiently, bursting through the swinging doors, shouting out lunch orders, glancing at the clock a hundred times an hour, muttering under his breath. Loretta grumbles under her breath, too, but for different reasons. She stands at the counter, shifting from one slow, bored foot to another, taking orders from the customers, yawning as they make their choices and sort through their wallets for the right money.

But Josh—Josh hums as he works. He chops onions, slices meats, stirs things in pans, his forehead knotted with concentration, his movements deliberate, economical. To look at him, you'd think he was taking all the time in the world—and yet he'll be finished making a focaccia before Loretta's even had time to spoon the froth onto a cappuccino. He exudes energy: a constant throb of it, warm, colorful, alive.

I watch the pelicans in the air, their wings stretched and pink-tipped from the sun. Then I say curiously, "Have you always liked cooking?"

He nods. "Even when I was a kid. I used to cook pancakes to cheer my mother up when she was feeling down. She'd eat them all up, right?—and then blame me for making her fat. Can you imagine?" He grins. "Then I got halfway through Year 11 and thought, hey, I'm onto something here. Cooking for people makes them feel good. Everyone likes food, right? And anyway, I hated school. So I left, and three weeks later I started my apprenticeship."

"What about your parents?" I ask him. "What did they say?"

"Oh, my mother hit the roof when she found out," he says, shrugging. "My stepdad was okay about it, though: he said it was good to get a trade. Anyway, they couldn't stop me."

I have to admit, I'm impressed. I can't imagine wanting to do anything so badly that I'd fight my parents over it, leave school for it. Well, I can't imagine wanting to do *anything* badly, period.

There is no way I could ever say this to him, of course. In fact, right now, looking sideways up at Josh next to me on the stone wall, I realize there's a whole *lot* I can't say. Like—the way his hand touching mine on the tap this afternoon made me feel. Like the way he seems so colorful, so full of conviction, so *driven*. Like how when he smiles, the freckles seem to dance on his face.

I take a deep breath and look away, back at the pelicans, which are floating now, their feet propelling them invisibly across the water. Next to me, Josh swings one leg back over the wall so that he's sitting sideways, facing me.

"Hey, Nat—"

"Yeah?"

He touches my knee, rests his hand there lightly. "What're you thinking about?"

I can feel my whole body stiffening again under his touch. "Nothing," I say quickly.

"Mmm," he says. "Yeah. *Right.*"

"It's true! I was miles away."

"So you *were* thinking about something." He smiles.

I don't answer.

His fingers brush across my cheek, once, twice. "Your face—" he says wonderingly.

My cheek tingles where he touched me. I open my mouth to speak.

"You've got such a beautiful face, Nat. So open. So *honest*."

I stare at him incredulously.

"You're hallucinating," I say gruffly. "You must've been drinking too much of that wheatgrass juice."

The freckles are dancing on his face again. "You reckon?"

"Everything has side effects, you know. Even wheatgrass."

"Then all I can say is, I *like* the side effects," Josh says, laughing, and he pushes the brocaded cap back on his head, leans over, and kisses me.

It isn't the first kiss I've ever had and it's not a long one. But his lips brush warm against mine, and his breath is sweet and close.

I'll *never* be able to wipe the grin off my face now. Tim, I am at your mercy.

chapter five

"Movie girl"

Josh doesn't call. All *week* he doesn't call. I hang around in my bedroom after school, not ringing Lise, not ringing Sofe, yelling at Tim if he heads for the phone. I'm *sure* I gave him my number.

By Saturday morning, I'm a mess. How the hell am I going to walk back into the Wild Carrot? Was it all just one big mistake?

I think about calling Michael, telling him I've quit. But I can't; I know I can't. This weekend is Easter—the busiest weekend of the year, he told me the other day. I can't just leave him in the lurch like that. Gloomily, I change into my work clothes and plod down to the tram stop.

But by the time I arrive, the café's already frantically busy. There is no time to talk to anyone; there's no time to do anything, in fact, except slip on my apron and get over to the cappuccino machine. Between frothing milk and clearing dirty tables, I barely even see Josh all morning.

By lunchtime there's a queue at the counter that stretches halfway to the door. People stand, waiting—hot, sticky, irritable in this last burst of intense autumn heat. In the kitchen, the exhaust fan hums, the fly-zapper snaps, the dishwasher shudders. Michael charges through the swinging doors every ten minutes, dumping piles of dirty plates in the middle of the sink, scattering knives and forks and scrumpled-up napkins all over my neatly stacked dishes: "Table one, table one, they've been waiting half an hour—"

I mutter imprecations at the sink. "He told me to stack the dirty plates *tidily,* and then what does he bloody well do himself?"

In the middle of all of this, Josh finally wanders over to me at the sink, dirty saucepan in his hand. My heart skids and thumps, just from looking at him. His apron is covered in grease and tomato stains, the cloth cap falling slightly to one side, and he's *humming* again. He looks askance at me as he puts the saucepan down on the draining board, his head to one side.

"You all right?"

It's the first time we've spoken to each other properly all morning—which makes it the first time since he kissed me last week at the tram stop. *Definitely,* I tell myself now, that kiss must have been a mistake.

"Nat?"

"Yeah. Yes. I'm *fine.*"

He laughs at the scowl on my face, clasps his hand around my wrist. "You need a movie tonight." His fingers stroke the inside of my wrist, slowly. "Nat? You're a movie girl, right?"

I swallow, hard. His fingers send shivers down my arm.

"I *love* movies," I admit finally, grudgingly. "Especially sci-fi."

"Sci-fi it is, then," he says, and moves back to the stove.

There is no explanation, no apology. No *Sorry I didn't call you, but—*

I should ask him, I tell myself over and over, staring at his back. *I should at least say something.* But it's no good: at the touch of his skin on mine, all my anger has just vanished.

I mean, what could I say, anyway? I'm just so glad it *wasn't* a mistake after all.

By the time I get off the tram on the way home after the movie, I'm just about *bursting* with happiness. I *have* to tell someone about my day. I'll call Sofe, I think, and grin wryly in memory at her comment about "men in uniform."

But when I walk through the back door, past the laundry room, and into the kitchen, Mum's there, waiting for me. (She knows, of course, where I've been: I rang after work to let them know I'd be home late, and got Dad on the phone.)

"How was it?" she asks eagerly. "What does he look like? Has he had a girlfriend before? How *old* is he?"

Something about her excitement instantly deflates me.

"It was good. He's nice. You'd like him."

"You'll have to have him over for dinner."

I groan. "*Mum.* I've only just *met* the guy."

She's always like this, my mother: she wants to know everything. When I was a kid, I used to confide in her heaps. She has that social worker's way of drawing things out of you, getting you to talk. Making you feel like she's your *friend,* not your mother.

But these days, it feels like the reason she asks all those questions is so that she can take my stories away from me and make them all right. Mum wants so desperately for everything to be all right for her kids; she longs for us to have happy endings. (The thing is, we generally do: just not always in the way she wants us to.)

"What about Lise?" she asks me now. "Does Josh like Lise? He's *got* to be all right if he likes Lise."

That's another thing about my mother: she has this weird thing about Lise. In fact, they have a weird thing about each *other.* When we were younger, I used to feel like Lise came over to see Mum, not me. Whenever she visited, Mum would come up the hallway to my room and stand in the doorway, chatting. She'd say something to Lise and Lise would answer, and the bizarre thing was, she wasn't shy about it. Maybe the social work stuff works better on Lise than on me; sometimes I've wondered if there are things she's told Mum that she hasn't even *mentioned* to me.

"Such a sweet girl," Mum would always say after Lise had gone. "I hope—I just hope—"

I don't know what she hoped.

Then again, Lise herself lost out in the mother stakes. She's what you call nervous, Mrs. Mawson. *Neurotic.* The kind of person who won't let her kids have pets because of the hair they'd shed on her furniture. Maybe it's hardly surprising Lise talks to Mum instead.

Anyway, whatever—as far as Mum's question about Josh goes, I've barely even *talked* to Lise about him.

I've tried. I started to tell her, one day, about the Wild Carrot Café—about Michael, and Loretta, and the milk that never froths. Then I said—just casually, you know?—"I've met this gorgeous guy there—"

"That's nice, Nat," she said distantly, not even waiting for me to finish.

I thought she might ask me for more details—*anything,* really: the color of Josh's eyes, or what his full name is, or what kind of food he cooks—but she didn't. She didn't ask a thing.

So I shut up. She made me feel kind of self-centered. *Childish,* almost.

Now, thinking about it, listening to Mum burble happily away at me in the kitchen, I realize that I've never really talked to Lise about this kind of stuff. Up until Year 11, I hadn't actually met anyone I was keen on. I'd had crushes on football players and actors, of course—but not anyone *real;* not anyone who was in my *life.* By the time that happened, Sofe had come along, and it's been her I've gossiped to about it ever since, not Lise.

What does Lise feel about me meeting Josh? I wonder. Is she excited for me? Or jealous? She could be bored, for all I know. I'd love her to tell me what she thinks; I'd love to know. I'd love to *share* this thing with her: what it feels like, finally, to be going out with a guy, how it's changed me, how it's changing my life. It is, you know. It really is.

The thing is, Lise and I have always shared the way we feel about things with each other. Suddenly not to be doing that feels wrong. Somehow, it feels *totally* wrong.

Mum thinks I told her everything about Josh today. In a way, of course, I did. I told her we'd been to a film, that it was fun, that I think Josh is great.

But the version I said out loud isn't the same as the memory inside my head.

"Let's break all those stereotypes," Josh said as we climbed up the carpeted stairs to the cinema. He grinned at me. "Let's *not* crackle our potato chip packets and *not* talk all the way through. We could even, you know, *watch* the film."

So we sat right down near the front of the theater, backs stiff, hands folded in our laps, politely licking at our ice cream cones. We didn't even whisper to each other during the ads.

Halfway through the movie, Josh's elbow slid across the arm of my seat. He took my hand in his, rested it gently on his thigh. I glanced across at him, but he was staring straight ahead at the screen as promised, his face rock-still. When I turned back to the screen, his thumb started to stroke the back of my hand.

My stomach fluttered helplessly. I sat there in the dark with him and, despite our vows, just *lost* the rest of the film.

I've never felt like that about anyone before: the way I felt when I was around Mario didn't even come close. (I mean, unlike Josh, for starters, Mario didn't feel anything for me.) It's a weird, wonderful, secret, *growing* feeling, and it's something I'd never tell my mother about—no matter how much she encourages me (or *pushes* me) to confide in her.

It's a feeling of knowing. That's what's so amazing about it. I just *know* I want him to be in my life.

Not just that: it feels like, now that I've met him, I know where I want my *life* to go.

chapter six

Out of uniform

At exactly 4:30 the next Saturday afternoon, Sofia walks into the café.

She's timed it perfectly. The last of the customers left a few minutes ago, and we've already finished most of the cleaning. The coffee shop has been quiet all day: it's cool and windy, which apparently doesn't help business; and besides, the customers are all practicing what Michael calls "post-Easter stinginess." I've spent the last couple of hours idly polishing glasses and wondering what Josh and I will do together tonight.

("We *will* do something, won't we?" I said to him in the kitchen this morning, anxiously. He was rummaging around in the fridge, and he looked up at me irritably to answer. "Of *course,* Nat; why *not*?" I don't think he realizes how unsure I still feel around him. Not about my feelings for him, I mean: what worries me is how he feels about *me.* I keep thinking I must've dreamt the whole thing up, you know?)

I don't actually see Sofe arrive because I'm out in the kitchen, putting the tea towels into a bucket of bleach to soak overnight. The first I know that she's here is when her voice, loud and cheerful, rings through the café: "Is it too late to get a coffee?"

I rush out. She's standing at the counter with a short, dreamy-looking ponytailed guy by her side. I look him over curiously. Is this the famous Aquatic Centre Nick?

Josh and Michael—who are out there with them already (they were stacking chairs on the tables when Sofia arrived)—also look intrigued.

"You know each other?" Josh asks me.

Hastily, Sofe and I make introductions. Michael shakes hands with Nick, nods at Sofia. Then he turns to me genially.

"Off you go, Nat. I was going to let you go in a few minutes, anyway."

I turn to Josh, suddenly uncertain. "I'll see you in a while, then . . . ?"

The minute the words are out of my mouth, I realize what I've done. I stare at Josh, mortified. *Don't tell Michael about us,* Josh warned me on the phone this week. *He thinks relationships between colleagues are unprofessional. You know how fanatic he is about work.*

Now Michael glances from Josh to me, and then back again. You can see his mind ticking over, making connections, going *click-click-click.* I feel myself blushing. Josh pulls faces at me frantically behind his back and pretends to slit his throat.

Finally, Michael turns once more to Josh.

"I guess you'd like to finish up now, too, mate."

It's a statement, not a question. Josh clears his throat, nods. "If that's all right."

Michael shrugs. Then, miraculously, he smiles. "Go on, then, the pair of you." He wags a scolding finger at us, and it's impossible to tell whether he's joking or not. "Just don't make a habit of this, all right? You *don't* have my blessing."

He watches us go, his arms folded across his chest. He doesn't say another word.

Outside, the sky looks threatening. Clouds loom over the sea at the end of the street, and the corner of an advertising poster on a streetlamp has come loose and flaps in the wind. We all look at each other, suddenly doubtful as our first idea—to go down to the beach—just kind of fizzles in front of us.

"Let's go and get some chips at the fish-and-chip shop and take them back to my place," Josh suggests. "None of you eats fish, right? I could fry up some eggs instead. There's nothing like fried eggs with chips."

It's the first time he's mentioned to me that he lives around here: up until now, I had no idea at all where his home was. In fact, it turns out that he lives in a townhouse a couple of roads back from the beach, on a side street on the other side of Jetty Road from the café. "A five-minute walk from here," he promises us on the way to the fish-and-chip shop.

Afterward, as we walk back to Josh's house, Sofe grabs me, makes me hang back with her while the other two walk on ahead.

"It's a happening thing, hey—you and Josh," she says. When I nod cautiously, she gives me a big, pleased grin: "He's nice, Nat. He's *cute.*"

You can say that again, I think, looking at his tall, narrow back ahead of us with a sudden flush of pride.

As he unlocks his front door, I take a deep breath before following the others in, my heart suddenly awash with happiness. I can't believe I'm here, in his house. I can't believe he asked us here; I can't believe he asked *me* here.

A moment later, Sofe, Nick, and I are settling ourselves in Josh's tiny living room while he bounds upstairs to his bedroom to get changed out of his work clothes. Coming back down again a couple of minutes later, he goes straight into the kitchen—which is separated from the living room by a row of waist-high cupboards—to fry the eggs. Nick has plopped himself on the sofa under the stairs, while Sofe and I sprawl out on the floor by his feet, gossiping away about school. Secretly, I'm spying on Josh while we chat: he's taken his cap off and is now wearing jeans and a T-shirt. Somehow his legs seem even longer and leaner than before, his cheekbones higher, his jawline squarer. He looks even *better* than he does in uniform, if you want to know the truth.

Nick listens to Sofe and me talking with a cheerful, disarming smile on his face. He's what you'd call laid-back, Nick: relaxed and easy to be with. He's studying arts,

Sofe told me recently—classics, philosophy, geography, a bit of astronomy: "Anything that sounds vaguely interesting, really, is how he puts it." She grinned as she told me this. "He's got no idea what he wants to do when he's finished. He's the *eternal* student."

When Josh comes back into the living room with the food a few minutes later, Sofe goes and perches on the arm of the sofa next to Nick, to eat. Smiling up at her, he takes her hand and rests it in his. It's a simple, natural gesture, you know? Not at all sleazy or possessive. He's *definitely* one of her better choices.

Josh, meanwhile, comes and sits cross-legged on the floor next to me.

"So what are you planning to do next year, after you've finished your apprenticeship, Josh?" Nick asks, with his mouth full. "You going to open a restaurant or something?"

Josh stops eating, his fork halfway to his mouth.

"I've got this dream of running a fast-food health café one day," he says. "Like an anti-McDonald's, right?"

"Why?" Sofe asks curiously.

He grimaces. "I *loathe* McDonald's. People go and buy their beefburgers and french fries and thickshakes there, and they don't even give a thought to all those trees cut down in the Amazon rain forests to make room for grazing beef cattle. I want to make people *think* about what they eat."

He has this emphatic way of speaking, Josh. You can tell when he's passionate about something from the vehemence in his voice, you know? Like now. What *is* it, I wonder idly, that makes him so urgent about something like the environment? And what would it feel like, to be so *certain*?

But I'm only half listening to the conversation, to tell the truth, letting the others toss it back and forth between themselves. I keep getting distracted by Josh: his gold-blond hair and dark brown eyes, and the way his bangs, long and thick, fall over his forehead as he talks. There is *no* cap line on that perfect head of hair. While the others debate the merits of beefburgers, I edge slowly, sneakily, closer toward him on the carpet. If I can just get a little nearer, our knees might touch—

Sofe puts her fork down on her plate with a clatter, and stretches luxuriously.

"That was great, Josh. Thanks."

She gets up from the sofa and starts to wander around the flat, looking curiously at things. On a small shelf over the gas heater, she finds a framed photo, which she picks up.

"Who's this?"

"My granddad," Josh says, pushing his empty plate away from him on the floor. "He died a few years ago."

"Really?" She shoots him a sympathetic look. "D'you miss him?"

He shrugs. "Sometimes. He was a bit of a stubborn old bugger. He lived in this big old house in the hills, and refused to drive anywhere. Said we were given legs to get around on, not wheels."

I reach over daringly and poke his thigh. "Now, who does *that* sound like?"

He has the grace to grin. "Yeah, my mother says I'm a lot like him. And I *don't* think she means it as a compliment."

Sofe's still standing by the heater, holding the photo.

"After my granny died," she says slowly, "I could have *sworn* I could feel her presence. For months afterward, I felt it."

"Like a ghost, you mean?" I ask, intrigued.

She looks thoughtful. "Sort of. But it was more like she was just *there.* I used to talk to her, ask her questions. Then one day she just vanished."

"Maybe she came to peace with her death," says Nick.

She smiles at him. "Yeah. Maybe."

Josh shifts restlessly next to me.

"Grief does strange things to your mind," he says abruptly.

We all turn toward him.

"Well, that's what it was, right?" he says, as if it's obvious. "It was Sofia coming to terms with her granny's death. That's all." He looks around at us unapologetically. "I don't believe in ghosts, or life after death, or spirits. It's all in the mind. It's New Age crap, basically."

The way he says it isn't rude, exactly: it's more *dismissive* than anything, I guess. Still, I'm surprised. Me, I'd be too afraid of hurting Sofe's feelings to put it quite so bluntly.

But she just shrugs.

"It's not New Age," she says to him matter-of-factly. "Granny was just *there.* I *know.*"

She does know, too. You can see it in her face. She has no doubts at all about what she's saying.

Josh looks at her long and hard. I watch him carefully, suddenly holding my breath. All at once, there's something going on between the two of them—something I can't quite interpret. Something weird. He *likes* her, I think, my heart sinking: I mean, *really* likes her. As in, now that he's met Sofe, he likes *her* and not *me.* He likes the way she challenges him, the way she holds her own.

Then I wonder why I'm so surprised. *All* the guys like Sofia better than me.

But when I examine him more closely, I realize that's not what it is at all. The expression on his face isn't one of admiration: in fact, it's one of dislike—strong, fast-growing dislike. As if he thinks she's *stupid* or something. I stare at him, astonished. *No* one dislikes Sofe.

"What do *you* reckon, Nat?" Josh says, looking away from her to me for support.

As he says this, his knee finally brushes against mine, and for a moment all I can feel is our knees touching through our clothes. Incredibly, he doesn't move away. I am instantly, helplessly paralyzed; for a moment, I can't even speak to answer him.

"I don't know," I say at last, looking honestly into his eyes. "I've never seen a ghost myself, but that doesn't mean they don't exist, you know?"

"Exactly," says Sofia.

She smiles at me, triumphant. But to tell the truth, I'm barely aware of her anymore, and Josh, too, appears to have forgotten her. He's looking at me, and me *only,* not bothering with the conversation about ghosts. In fact, he's stopped talking altogether. Our knees stay touching, and his eyes bathe my face, and I am warmed all over by those eyes. I feel like I'm *glowing.*

You know what? I could bask forever like this under his gaze. *Totally* forever.

Afterward—long afterward, when Nick and Sofe have gone and Josh and I have fooled around in the kitchen for as long as we can, pretending to wash the dishes—he offers to walk me back to the tram.

I hesitate, not wanting, despite everything, to make assumptions.

"You don't have to. I can get there by myself. I mean, I'm not trying to *force* you—"

He shakes his head, squeezes my elbow. "Don't you think I *want* to?" He puts his finger on my nose, presses it teasingly. "You're *not* forcing me, Nat, okay?"

Outside, in the street, we walk together for a few moments, not talking. Josh's steps are long and loping; without saying anything, he shortens them so that I can keep up. I smile up at him gratefully, and he smiles back, and for some reason this reminds me of the totally *unsmiling* way he looked at Sofia earlier in the evening.

"You don't have much use for Sofe, do you?" I say as we wait at the traffic lights.

"She's all right, I guess." He pauses. "I'm sorry, Nat. I know she's your friend. I'm just not *into* all that spiritual stuff."

I think about this.

"She had a pretty hard childhood, you know? Her parents split up when she was a kid, and now her mum's a single mother."

"And?" he says, like this has no relevance to what we're talking about at all.

"And—well—"

He sighs impatiently. "She's not the only kid in the world whose parents split up, you know."

"I know." I take a breath, wanting to stay loyal to her. "I just think it's good that she's so positive. I think it's good she *believes* in stuff."

He doesn't say anything for a while. We reach the roundabout in front of the hotel, cross over to the terminus. There's a tram waiting there already, its engine off, the driver sitting inside, reading a paper. Josh and I go and stand outside the cement shelter, under the streetlamp.

"My parents split up, too," he says, finally. He looks away from me, puts his hands in his pockets. "I was ten years old. My dad started screwing around with this woman from work when I was seven. It went on for three years."

"Three *years*?"

"Oh, everyone knew about it," he says bitterly. "I knew; the kids at school knew; the neighbors knew. *Mum* knew." He crosses his arms against his chest, looking at the ground. "She went around with this stupid, wet look on her face for three years. She used to burst into tears at the drop of a hat. And then, when Dad finally said he was going to leave her, she had a *nervous breakdown*."

I swallow. "So what happened?"

"She got married again when I was thirteen," he says flatly. "She's been with Greg ever since."

I hesitate, not knowing what to say. "Is he nice, your stepdad?"

He frowns. "He's *stable.* He loves her. He has a *mortgage.* That's all my mother wants now. I don't think she actually loves him; she just tells herself she does."

He falls quiet then, moving restlessly out of the pool of orange light from the streetlamp to lean his back against the cement wall of the tram shelter. His long legs stretch out in front of him, and his face is suddenly obscured by darkness.

"The best thing I ever did," he says, "was leave home. Move out into my home by the beach. Get my own life."

He shifts again, moving his weight from one foot to the other. I think about saying something, decide against it. There's something in his face that tells me, just for now, to keep quiet.

"My mother is a weak, stupid woman, Nat," he says at last, shrugging. "She's too scared to find out the truth, so she lies to herself. I *despise* people who lie to themselves."

Something about his words shocks me. It's not *what* he's saying, exactly; it's more, I think, the way he says it. There's this note of real withering scorn in his voice, his eyes, when he talks about his mother. I have to admit, I don't like it. It's like the stuff he said to Sofia earlier, the impatient way he dismissed her beliefs. He's so passionate about his own convictions, it's like there's no room for anyone else's; no room for anything other than black and white.

But I think what strikes me most is his *bitterness.* Listening to him at moments like this, you don't get any sense of optimism. Me, I like to look at the bright side of things. In that way—in that one way, at least—I'm totally my mother's daughter. I mean, you can hate life or you can love it, you know? So you might as well love it.

Then again, maybe if I'd had parents like Josh's . . .

The tram, waiting silently on the tracks next to us, shudders suddenly into life, its engine warming up for the trip back to the city. The driver climbs out for one last cigarette, leaving the engine running. Behind us, beyond the tram stop, lies the beach. The sea is slick and silvery in the moonlight.

Josh pushes himself away from the wall of the shelter, turns to me.

"I'm sorry. I didn't mean to get so heavy." His voice is husky and quiet. He puts a hand on my shoulder, his thumb stroking my collarbone. "I'm not always like that."

When he touches me, I forget everything else. My whole body buzzes and hums. If you attached a battery to me, I'd send out sparks, switch on lights.

"Sweet Nat," says Josh softly, and cups my chin with his hand.

The tram engine throbs. Josh kisses me, and his lips taste faintly of salt carried in on the sea air. We move in toward each other, shutting out the cool evening breeze between us. I can feel his warmth, his urgency, and I like it. I lap it up—all that color, that energy of his; all the strength of his feelings. Good *and* bad.

The tram driver throws his cigarette away, gets into the tram. We break apart.

"I'll call you," Josh says to me as I climb into the tram.

All the way home, I lean my head against the smeared window, close my eyes, taste him on my lips.

The thing about Josh: he makes me feel so—*alive.*

PART II

Lise

chapter seven

"Crybaby"

One thing you need to know about me: I never cry. Not at sad movies, not at sad books, not at TV; not even when I feel sick, or premenstrual, or down. I just *don't cry.*

When I was little, I cried all the time. My sister Terri was always teasing me about being a crybaby, and the name sort of stuck; sometimes, when I screwed up my face after my father had told me off, he'd say, with an impatience that was unusual for him, "*Christ,* Lise, don't be such a crybaby."

Crybaby *Lise.* I hated that name, hated what it represented. *Weak,* that's what I was. A *sniveler.* So finally, in Year 7, I made a New Year's resolution not to cry anymore. And, just like that—overnight—I stopped. I don't think I've cried again since.

Except once. A couple of years ago, on my fourteenth birthday, my parents gave me a portable CD player. It was a Sony, with double CD deck, radio, detachable speakers, remote control, the works.

"It's fantastic," Nat said enviously when she came over later that day.

I sat on my bed, back against the wall, knees to my chest, watching her fiddle around with all the knobs. I couldn't bear to join in; I hadn't yet touched it myself.

"It cost heaps," I told Nat. "I saw it in an ad on TV last week."

"It leaves my Walkman for *dead*."

I said nothing to this. I turned my face to the wall, rested my cheek on my knee. My throat burned with shame.

"Have you listened to it yet, Lise?"

"No."

"Can I try it out?"

"If you really want to . . ."

She went out to the living room, pinched a CD from my parents' collection. When she came back and put it on, the air in my bedroom soared instantly with the unbearable, sweet sadness of violins and pianos.

"Wow," Nat said simply. "Even Tchai-bloody-kovsky sounds good on this."

You could hear the timpani in the background, like the roll of a wave in the sea. *Oh, God.* I swallowed, hard. *Don't cry, don't cry, don't cry . . .*

"Don't you like it?" asked Nat.

I lifted my head then, to answer. "I told you. I saw how much it cost."

"So?"

"So," I said throatily. "Nobody *else's* parents spend that much money on them for their fourteenth birthday."

Nat looked puzzled. "Well, you're just lucky, then."

A tear spilled over my cheek.

"It's *too much,*" I said, sniffing.

Nat switched the stereo off. The violins stopped indignantly in mid-string.

"*Lise.* They love you. They can afford it. Why *not*?"

"Because . . . ," I said, my voice cracking. "Because I don't *want* an expensive present. I don't want to be the lucky one. I don't want the *responsibility.*"

Nat tried, bewildered, to hug me, but I pushed her arms away, turned my face once more to the wall. Ashamed, yes—but of what, I don't know. Of my tears, perhaps, or of the feelings behind them.

It's the only time I can remember crying since I've been in high school. The only time Nat's ever seen me cry.

Part of me is proud of it, I suppose—the not crying. Of the self-control it takes, the discipline. And of the *strength* . . .

chapter eight

In the mirror

A couple of Saturdays after Easter, it's Terri's eighteenth birthday.

She's bubbling from the moment the doorbell rings and the first of her uni friends arrives, at eight o'clock. She flits around from room to room in her new party dress, dimples dancing in her cheeks, wineglass in hand. She lights candles everywhere and turns up the music on the stereo notch by notch until my father exchanges glances with my mother and says, "I think it's time we went out for that bite to eat."

Mum nods. "You coming, Lise?"

Terri wafts into my bedroom as I'm brushing my hair hurriedly, conscious of Dad drumming his fingers in the car. She gives me a pitying look, magnanimous with birthday happiness.

"Why don't you stay, Lise?" she says. "You don't *really* want to go out with Mum and Dad, do you?"

She comes over to me in front of the mirror, throws her arms around my shoulders, croons into my ear.

"C'mon, Lisa-lou, stay and have some fun . . ."

I look at her slender, flushed, happy face next to mine in the mirror. *Fun.* Terri always calls me "Lisa-lou" when she's trying to coax me into being different. Happy, maybe, or . . . *normal.* She doesn't seem to realize that that's never going to happen, no matter how much she wants it to. No matter how much *I* want it to.

I shrug my shoulders free of her clasp, scowl at her in the mirror.

"I *am* having fun," I tell her, and run out to the garage, where the engine is already growling impatiently.

In the restaurant, Mum fusses over the menu ("I'll have the fish grilled, not fried, please. And just steamed vegetables, thank you. No butter") while Dad swirls the ice cubes in his Scotch good-humoredly. He's happy: it's his weekend off being on call, which means he can drink. The red wine that comes out with the main course is his favorite.

"Dessert, ladies?" he says gallantly as the waitress clears our plates.

Mum shakes her head, already fingering her cigarette lighter underneath the table. *I don't eat dessert,* she always tells everyone virtuously. (And she doesn't—not unless you count the chocolate bar she stashes away "for energy" in her handbag, alongside her cigarettes.) She orders a cappuccino, and shoots me a surreptitious disapproving look across the table when I decide on some sticky date pudding.

Dad smiles at me genially. "That's right, Lisey. You enjoy yourself," he says, and orders a slice of cheesecake for himself.

She's right, though, I think guiltily as I spoon up caramel sauce and cream. I've kept so well, this week, to the diet I set myself over the Easter break, and now I'm breaking all my rules. It's just . . . I don't want to go home yet. I *really* don't want to go back home.

I should have organized to go and see Nat tonight, slept over at her place. Avoided Terri's party altogether. And a year ago, that's exactly what I would have done, but now . . . I don't know. We went out together to the movies the other night, but before that, it had been *ages* since we did anything outside of school. Sometimes, these days, it's hard to believe that we even live close to each other.

Besides, let's face it, I think bitterly: Nat would probably rather spend the time with her boyfriend now than with me.

Mum drives home, her foot jerking on and off the accelerator constantly, the way it always does when she's stressed—or when, like tonight, she's annoyed about having to drive home because Dad's over the limit.

"They'll have to leave by midnight. You *did* tell Terri everyone would have to leave by midnight, Rob . . ."

In the warm, cushioned darkness of the car, Dad sighs. "Yes, love. I told her."

"Because I've got that open house scheduled for nine tomorrow." The car rocks forward, pulls back, in sickening tempo with her foot. "It's the Darleys' house—the one that's been on the market for two months now. I really can't afford a bad night's sleep."

Dad fingers the knob on the radio, turning the volume up ever so slightly before he settles back into his seat, head comfortably against the headrest.

"Don't worry about it, Jen, okay? I'll remind Terri again when we get back. You go straight to bed."

But after she has disappeared upstairs into their bedroom, he makes no visible effort to seek my sister out in the crowded living room at the other end of the house. And, like me, he seems unwilling to go to bed yet. He takes off his shoes and putters around the kitchen in his stocking feet, making himself a hot chocolate, smiling amicably at the odd guest passing through on their way to the ice-filled drink bucket in the laundry room. He spoons sugar and cocoa into a mug, adds milk, opens the microwave door.

"You sure you don't want one of these, Lisey?"

I shake my head quickly. No more sweet things. Got to get back to my diet. Got to get rid of that puppy fat.

On the way out, Dad hesitates in the kitchen doorway, mug in one hand. He glances over at me sitting on a barstool at the kitchen countertop. When I was little, he'd have come over and ruffled my hair, or tickled my tummy to make me laugh. *One step, two step, and a ti-ckle-y under there!*

I look away deliberately; pick up one of Mum's *Vogue*s; start reading it, head down.

"Good night, then, honey," he says after a moment. His voice has that same wistful, puzzled note it's had ever since he stopped being able to make Terri and me squeal with delight at his efforts. Sometimes he sounds so disappointed, I feel as if I've let him down, somehow, by growing out of his jokes.

When I don't look up, he pads with soft, sad feet up the stairs to the bedroom.

I flick idly through the glossy pages of the magazine. It's eleven o'clock; it'll be close to one, I'd say, before the last of Terri's friends leaves. The kitchen yawns—empty, silent—in contrast to the cheerful bubble of noise that drifts out from behind the closed living room door. What would it be like to be the kind of person who likes parties? I wonder. The kind of person who likes dancing, knows all the latest hits, doesn't care about school the next day? Who, like Terri, looks great in hipster jeans and crop tops . . .

On the wall opposite the stainless steel countertop there's a mirror, large and square-shaped, with a wrought-iron frame. (Mum chose it to match the legs of the barstools.) Out of the corner of my eye, I catch the movement of my reflection as I turn over the pages of the magazine.

"Don't you *hate* that mirror?" Nat said to me once, a couple of years ago. "I mean, doesn't it bother you, looking up in the middle of dinner and staring at yourself in the mirror—chewing?"

Now I look up, straight at myself. As always, a pale, blue-eyed face stares back at me, framed with long, messy, uncontrollable brown hair.

Could that ever be the face of someone who likes parties? Could anyone ever be fooled into *thinking* it was the face of someone who likes parties?

But the blue eyes stare back at me, inscrutable, giving away no answers.

And that's just it. I've never been able to read my face the way others read it; never been able to see whatever it is other people see there. That thing they see in my face which makes people like Sofia—people like my sister, people like my *mother*—shrug exasperatedly and walk away.

In my bedroom, I lie down, switch off the light, draw the curtains tightly to shut out the light from the streetlamp outside my window. My room is directly above the living room, and the voices coming from down below sound muffled, almost distant.

Still happy, though, those voices. You can muffle words, but not happiness.

I close my eyes, try to relax, to concentrate. I read this book recently about creative visualization. If you can just visualize what you want to change about yourself, the book said, you can make it happen, no matter what it is or how unattainable it seems. Even something like losing weight, or being happy, or passing your exams.

Ever since I read that book, I've been putting it into practice every night before I go to sleep. You've got to start somewhere, after all. But the problem is, sometimes I can't sleep for trying to decide what I should try to visualize that night.

Because that's the point. There are *so many* things about myself I want to change.

And none of these things seems attainable.

chapter nine

The way things change

"So how's things going with that hunky chef of yours?" says Sofia to Nat one lunchtime a couple of weeks later.

We've just come in from underneath the Moreton Bay fig tree after a short, sharp shower. This week we've had the first of the autumn rains; the sky's turned low and gray, and months of cold, wet dreariness stretch ahead of us. The rec room, heated by the school's geriatric oil heating system, is fuggy with the smell of hot chips and microwaved meat pies. Fragments of loud, cheerful, inane conversation drift over to us as we talk. ("What did you get for question four in the math test?" "Go on—have another one. You're so *skinny*." "Anyway, so get this—he asked me *out*.")

Nat looks dreamily out the window, not answering Sofe's question straightaway.

"Things're good," she says. "Great. I mean—okay." She blushes.

"So—have you two *done it* yet?" Sofia asks.

"Sofe." She colors again.

"Well, *have* you?"

"What about you and Nick?" Nat counters. "Or have you already broken up with him?"

"Actually," says Sofia, "we're still together."

And it's weird, but there's the same dreamy look about her that Nat had a moment ago—only there's something else in her face, too. She's more certain, more confident about it, somehow, than Nat.

Nat turns to me, gaping. "How many weeks do you make that, Lise?"

I count back. "Eight weeks. No—nine. That's two whole months!"

We stare at Sofia in astonishment. This is a record: as far as I can remember, Sofe's never gone out with a boy for longer than a month.

Nat says slowly, "This is, like—*serious.*"

And Sofia nods, her eyes glowing. "I know."

Things are changing. More and more, I look around me at moments like this and I realize that everyone in my life is changing, moving on. And there's nothing I can do about it. No matter how much I try to forget it, ignore it, deny it, that's what's happening.

I feel so far behind, so out of sync.

When I first met Nat, at the beginning of Year 7, we were both new girls, stiff and uncertain in our starchy green school dresses. After Assembly, we got back to our home-room and our teacher, Mrs. Botticelli, had assigned us desks next to each other. I put my books and pens and rulers down on my desk. I didn't know what to say, was terrified of this big-boned, straight-brown-haired, freckled girl sitting next to me. But Nat just turned and smiled at me—a cheerful, open, slightly gap-toothed smile—and said, "I *hate* being new. Don't you?"

And I knew, from that moment, that things would be all right as long as she was around.

Being friends with Nat was easy. It was pure luck, of course—I knew that even then—but it just felt so *right*. We went on trips to Glenelg at the end of each summer holiday: lay on the sand in the sun, rubbed sunblock on each other's shoulders, told secrets in the lull of the sea. On weekends we made cakes at her house for afternoon tea, rode our bikes to the supermarket for candy, caught the bus into town to go to the movies.

And I thought I was safe. I thought that maybe, after all, things would be all right; that life would be good (as Nat's mother always says). I told myself that perhaps I'd gotten over the worst bit. For years, I told myself that.

But then things started to change.

In Year 11, Sofia came to our school. From the moment she came up to us one lunchtime with her free, loping stride and said, "Mind if I sit with you?" I knew I'd been wrong about being safe. About being over the worst bit.

Sofia, with the cigarette packet in her uniform chest pocket; Sofia, with the ponytail that swings as she walks; Sofia, who says "*Mate,* it's hot" and "*Mate,* he's cool" and

"*Mate,* I'm stuffed." Right from the start, Sofe made Nat laugh in a way she never used to before; and she talked to Nat about boys, sex, condoms—all the things I can't talk about. Nat was interested; she listened, answered, laughed.

So I knew straightaway—guilty about the way it made me feel, of course, but still knowing it was true—that their friendship was going to change everything. That just by Sofia being there, things had changed; and that they'd go on doing so, no matter what I felt about it.

But it's not just Sofe, to be fair. There are other things, too—like Nat's new job, for example. Now, instead of ringing me up on Saturday morning and saying, "Hey, you want to go and have a gelato at Alfresco's?" she puts on her uniform (black jeans and an unbleached cotton T-shirt with carrots dancing wildly all over it) and catches the tram to Glenelg for the day. She loves that job; she's walked around with a permanent smile on her face ever since she got it.

She tried to talk to me about it the other day. She started to tell me this story about working there, and I think what she was really trying to tell me about was her boyfriend, Josh. But I didn't know how to answer her. I wondered, too, why she was telling me, what the point of it was. What do *I* know about falling in love? What could I say? We've never talked about it before. I felt ashamed of my lack of experience, my lack of *feeling.*

It's not that I'm not happy for her, because I am. I know how much she wanted to get a job, and I'm glad it's turned out so well for her. It's just that . . . I miss her.

Now, sitting in the rec room with Nat and Sofe, I think, how can you miss someone you see practically every day? Someone who lives around the corner from you; someone who's sitting right here next to you? It doesn't make sense. But . . . I don't know. It's as if, even when Nat's talking to me, she's somewhere else; as if she's absent, gone away. Won't come back.

We used to be so close, Nat and I.

Just as I'm thinking this, she waves her hand in front of my face. "Wakey, wakey, Lise—anyone home?"

I take a breath, shake myself inside. "Sorry—miles away."

She grins, rummages around in her schoolbag, digs out a packet of Tim Tams. "These'll bring you back to us."

Oh, no.

She grabs a couple of cookies and hands the packet over to Sofia, who takes one and offers them to me. I can smell them from here, their chocolate melting slightly in the warmth of the room. My mouth waters, and I can half taste them in my imagination.

"No, thanks," I say quickly, shaking my head.

"You *love* Tim Tams!" Nat protests.

"No, I don't," I say staunchly.

"You *do.* You told me you hated your mum because she wouldn't let you have any for afternoon tea. Remember?"

"Ages ago, maybe," I say casually. "Not anymore."

This takes great willpower, but I *have* to say no. I have no choice. Tim Tams are off-limits for me at the moment.

Because I've finally become serious about losing weight.

It's not just Tim Tams: I've decided that all snacks and treats are off-limits—even, sadly, cappuccinos. (Do you know how many *calories* there are in a cappuccino?) Breakfast, lunch, tea—that's all I eat now. I mean, why not? If I can stick to being vegetarian, I can stick to my diet. Surely. After all, that sticky date pudding a couple of weeks ago was the last "bad" thing I ate. Maybe creative visualization does work.

I still haven't told anyone about it, of course. They'd only fuss; they'd only come out with that old, old line, "But why do you want to go on a diet? You're not fat!"

Well, no, I'm not fat. Size 12 isn't fat. But it's not thin, either.

Three meals a day: the books and magazines all make it sound so easy. But it's not. It's hard; I hadn't imagined it could be so hard. The worst thing is, there are so many hours between each meal. I never noticed before how many hours there are. And I get so *hungry.*

But guess what? It's working already. When I weighed myself this morning, I realized I've lost a few pounds. Which means all I have to do is . . . keep going. Keep saying no.

Sometimes I think there isn't anything I'm really good at. I'm hopeless at sports, so-so at music, have to work my guts out to get those famous good marks at school. And it's not as if I'm popular or pretty, either, which might make up for all of that. So I just keep thinking, anyone can be thin if they try hard enough. I read somewhere that being thin's not a matter of genes; it's just discipline. *Will.*

If that's all it is, I can do it. I *have* to do it. I know it won't make everything okay—I'm not that stupid; I know I'll be the same person, the same old Lise. But . . . I don't know. At least if I'm thin I'll have something I can be proud of myself for, something I can *like* about myself.

And of all the things I want, of all the things in my life I'd like to change if only I could, this is something I *can* change.

This is something I can *do.*

chapter ten

Rules

The Fear slithers over me just as I turn the first page of the history test.

It comes from nowhere, this feeling. It's a feeling of panic, of *dread,* that curls and coils in my stomach. I focus on the blackboard, take a deep breath. *There's nothing to be afraid of. Get back to your test.*

I pick up my pen, bend my head back over the paper, and a wave of sickness crawls up my throat. I swallow once, twice; take another long, struggling breath. Keeping the sickness at bay. I grip my fingers around my pen with mad, determined tightness. *Write. Just write.*

Under the table, my knees start to tremble. The trembling goes all the way through my body; even my breath starts to shake. Sweat breaks out on my forehead, under my arms, on the top of my lip. There's a hotness in my throat again—only this time I can't swallow.

Come on. Come on. Calm DOWN.

I gulp in air. Gulp. Gulp. My heart beats rapidly, getting faster. Fear—black, irrational, uncontrollable fear—swells inside me.

God, oh, God, ohgodohgodohgod—

The first time this happened—the first time the Fear hit—was during the end-of-year exams last year. For a whole fifteen minutes during the last exam, I sat there, swallowing, shaking, convinced I was going to throw up or pass out. I thought I'd never make it through that exam.

And I still don't know, really, what made the feeling go away that afternoon. After a while, I remember, I began to breathe more easily; my heart slowed down. I picked up my pen and started writing again. I was exhausted; all I wanted to do, afterward, was go to sleep. I remember, too, how strange my writing on the paper looked when the teacher handed our exams back a week later. It looked nothing like my usual small, firm letters. This writing was faint, scrawly, out of control.

That was the lowest mark I've ever gotten on an exam. Oh, I passed, but . . . it wasn't anywhere near the kind of mark I usually get.

The thought that this might happen to me again has terrified me ever since.

And I've tried so hard, this year, to make sure it wouldn't. A couple of weeks ago, sometime around Easter, I wrote myself out a study schedule, pinned it up on the corkboard above my desk at home. One hour of studying in the morning, before school, and three hours after school, at home.

On the weekends, I study from nine to five on Saturday, and nine to one on Sunday.

The other day, Terri wandered into my bedroom and came over to my desk, where I was sitting, trying to do a math assignment. Her eyes darted up to the corkboard, and she read my schedule.

"What're all those colored marks? The ones in pink and green highlighter pen?"

"Pink's for when an essay's due. Green's for tests. And the blue one's for free time."

"Christ, Lise. There's only one blue mark a *week*."

"Yeah—but it *is* the whole of Sunday afternoon."

"But *why*? Why d'you want to study so much?"

I shrugged. "It's Year 12."

She stared at me. "Are you mad? I was lucky if I got any studying done at *all* on the weekend when I was in Year 12. And as for before school—wouldn't you rather be in bed?"

Yeah, right, Terri. It's okay for her to say that; she doesn't *need* to study. Terri could have passed Year 12 with her hands tied behind her back. Unfortunately, I'm just not that smart.

What I've been thinking is, if I study harder, I'll get better marks, so I'll be less worried. Which means there won't be any reason to feel the Fear.

I've stuck to it, too, that schedule. Religiously. So why, *why* am I feeling like this now? Why is it happening all over again?

★ ★ ★

But there have *always* been feelings like this.

In Year 5, right at the end of the year, my best friend, Sally, left the state. Her family moved to Perth just after Christmas. We'd been friends for years.

Year 6 was the worst year of my life. I didn't make friends again. I don't know why; I just . . . didn't. I felt so alone, so silent. Waves of sickness and Fear used to wash over me as I trudged, head down, through the endless school corridors. I spent my lunchtimes out behind the art room, reading, and on rainy days I went to the school library and helped Mrs. Birchill, the school librarian, with the reshelving. She was the only person I could talk to (even if it *was* just about books and the weather). I'm sure she was just nice to me because she felt sorry for me.

I've always been shy. I don't know why; I just *am*. But after Year 6, I stopped believing people could even *like* me; and, except for Nat, I've never been able to change my mind about that. I don't know . . . People didn't like me then, so why would they like me now? I haven't changed.

And even with Nat, I've always known, in my heart, that it wouldn't last. Sofia's arrival just proved me right.

Once, in one of my primary school reports, one of my teachers wrote: *Lise tries almost too hard*. I've never understood that comment. I thought that trying, making an effort, was a good thing. Besides, you *have* to try hard—to do well, to be liked, to be attractive. If you stop trying . . .

well, then people see who you *really* are. And they don't like you.

The other thing is, the shyness is worse—much worse—with boys. I clam up in the company of them, go as stiff as a board. For one thing, I don't have any experience of boys: I've never spent any time with them. At home, there's just Terri and me. All my cousins live out of state; my parents aren't friends with any of the neighbors; and, of course, I go to an all-girls school.

But it's not just that. Boys don't like me. Instinctively they don't like me, I mean. They look at my face, and—even more than most people—they see something in it that makes them walk away. I tell myself it's because I don't wear trendy clothes or makeup; because my stupid curly hair won't stay tied up; because I've got big thighs and a flabby stomach. Let's face it—I'm not exactly Miss Australia.

"Just don't *worry* about it, Lise," Nat said to me impatiently the last time we talked about it. "Sofe's not exactly a model, either, and look at *her* record with guys."

"They think I'm ugly," I said, trying to explain. "And fat. And . . . *boring*."

"Well, of course they'll think you're boring if you don't say anything," she said, exasperated. "Who wants to talk to a brick wall?"

When she saw the look on my face, she was horrified. She almost fell over herself trying to apologize.

"I didn't mean it like that! I *didn't*. I just meant—*relax*. Just be yourself, and everything'll be okay."

But that's my point. *Brick wall.* That's exactly what I am. I couldn't have put it better myself.

Other girls seem to follow all these complicated unwritten rules I don't know anything about. With boys, especially . . . but with other things, too. They just seem to *know* what to wear, what to say, how to act. It comes naturally to them, somehow; it's something they were born knowing.

And I feel so awkward, so heavy, so out of place. Sometimes I think that if I knew the rules—if I could learn them somehow—I'd be all right.

But it's not just that I'd be all right. If I knew all the rules, I'd be *normal.*

chapter eleven

Running

As the rain grows heavier and the wind gets colder—as we wrap up in our tartan winter-uniform skirts and blazers—I take up running.

There's no doubt about it: exercise helps you lose weight. I've lost ten pounds now, since Easter—which is more than I've ever managed to lose in my life. Even my mother, who's the queen of dieting (that is, the queen of yo-yo dieting), would be proud of that number. And people have started to notice, believe it or not. For the first time ever, I'm getting all these *compliments.*

One day in the rec room, even Sofia says, "Being vegetarian really seems to suit you, Lise. You look great." Then she grins, leans over to me, and whispers conspiratorially, "So tell me your *secret,* Miss Mawson."

I've lost ten pounds . . .

"I don't know," I lie. "Maybe all those lentils and tofu *are* good for you after all."

"Hmm," she says, a look of distaste crossing her face. "Think I'll stick to pasta and cheese."

The bell rings then, three times. I stand up, stretch, glance out the window.

"Look at the way Miss Stirling runs," I say to Nat and Sofia, pointing through the window across the schoolyard to a figure hurrying toward the staff room.

"Late again—"

"The woman's always in a rush."

"No, but look at the way she *runs,*" I say impatiently, trying to get my point across. "She barely lifts her feet off the ground. No wonder she's such a pathetic gym teacher."

Nat empties orange peels out of her lunchbox into the rubbish bin. "Since when are *you* the expert on running?"

"I run," I say indignantly, before I can stop myself. "Every morning, before breakfast."

Sofia and Nat look at me in astonishment.

"You must be joking."

"Since when?"

I can see what they're thinking. Is this *Lise* we're talking to? Round, lazy Lise, who took up piano in Year 11 so she could avoid after-school athletics?

"It's *good* for you," I say crossly, and walk away.

But the other thing about exercise, apparently, is that it kills your appetite. That's what all the health magazines say. I have to admit, I thought that was as good a reason as any to get serious about it.

What gave me the idea to take up running—as opposed

to something else, I mean, like swimming or cycling—was Nat's mother. I was over there one day a few months ago and Mrs. Jordan came into Nat's bedroom to say hello. She stood in the doorway, chatting, asking me how I was, what was going on in my life—all the things she usually asks me when I'm over. She was dressed in shorts and a T-shirt, and she had a headband around her forehead, so I asked her if she was going off somewhere to play sports. The question just came out, without me even thinking about it. It's always been like that for me with Nat's mother: I've never felt remotely shy with her. I don't know why. Somehow, she's just so easy to talk to.

"I'm going for a run," she told me, in answer to my question.

I was surprised. "I didn't know you were a runner."

"I used to run marathons when I was younger," she said. Then she sighed. "I'm not supposed to run at all now, really. Bad knees—from all those marathons, no doubt. But sometimes I just miss it. Running makes you feel so *good*."

So this year, when I decided it was finally time for me to get fit, running was the first thing I thought of.

At first I hated it. I couldn't get my breath, had to keep stopping and starting as I passed through the streets that follow the tramlines. It was so *cold,* too. The mornings are freezing now: your breath floats ahead of you in a cloud, and your skin goes all rubbery and pink. I couldn't *believe* how unfit I was.

But then one day I found my rhythm. As simple as that.

And it's the most amazing feeling. Now I know exactly what Mrs. Jordan was talking about.

These days, it's the part of the day I most look forward to. I set my alarm for half past five, get up at twenty-five to, change into my track pants, and have a glass of water on my way out through the kitchen. I jog slowly to the end of our street, warming up, then turn the corner and speed up as I head toward the bread bakery on the corner of the main road.

My route goes along tree-lined avenues by the tramline, past Italian people's houses with backyards full of grape-vines, and ramshackle stone cottages rented out to uni students and people on the dole. There's a little brown dog that sleeps on the porch of a corrugated-iron cottage on the street where I turn around to go back home; he always wakes as I run past, and shakes himself. By the time I come past him on the way back, he's waiting at the tin fence at the end of the driveway, his wet black nose poked, quivering, through the gap between the bottom of the gate and the cement. I was scared of him at first—I've always been a little afraid of dogs—till I realized he only wanted to see who I was.

The thing I like about running: it's the only time my mind switches off, feels quiet. It's as if, for once, I'm in tune with myself. As if the world has retreated and there's just me and this rhythm: the rhythm of my feet on the pavement. It's almost like meditating.

By the time I come back, the bakery's always well into

its working day. The aroma of baking bread fills the air; it's the most delicious, tempting smell. It makes me think of the crusty white loaves my mother went through a phase of making when Terri and I were little, before she started working full-time. She'd sprinkle them with sesame seeds and give them to us fresh out of the bread machine. And we'd sit cross-legged on the kitchen floor, tearing the bread into huge chunks, chewing and swallowing, chewing and swallowing. No matter how much you ate, you always wanted more.

Every time I run back past the bakery, I think about this; and every time, I tell myself I should run home another way. The smell's almost *too* good; it makes my knees go weak and my stomach rumble. I slow down and take deep breaths, filling my lungs with the warmth and the sweetness of it. *Just as good as eating it,* I tell myself as I turn the corner onto our own street.

But the moment I reach the entrance to our white-walled two-story house, the good feeling inside of me vanishes. I stop just inside the high wrought-iron gate; do a few hamstring stretches and lunges, trying to ignore the feeling of slow dread that creeps over me. Then I trudge up the gravel driveway, past Mum's real estate sign at the front (positioned so that people will see her name and phone number as they drive past). When I get to the back door, I walk through, hot and breathless, and Dad's standing there in the kitchen, doing up the buttons on his shirt, his pager beeping furiously.

The worst way of all to end the morning is when Terri's there, too, yawning cheerfully over a mug of coffee at the countertop, telephone already cupped between her shoulder and her ear. Even in her baby-blue terry-cloth bathrobe, her eyes still puffy from sleep, she looks gorgeous. She has straight blond hair; long, slim tennis player's legs; and eyelashes that look as if they've got permanent (unsmudgeable) mascara on them. I can still remember a colleague of my dad's gazing at Terri and me across the dinner table one evening, years and years ago, and saying, in this faintly amazed voice, "They're just so . . . *different.* You'd never guess they were sisters."

He was right, of course. And it's not just looks, either. When she was at school, Terri was one of those students that private schools dream of: she was a straight-A girl, a member of the varsity tennis team and junior varsity field hockey, a good enough piano player to be picked for every music competition, an elected student council rep in Year 12. In fact, she was—*is*—the kind of person with so many talents and gifts that you'd expect a little selfishness, a little arrogance, in her, as a matter of course.

But that's the thing about Terri that I find most difficult of all, even though I know I shouldn't. Because she just doesn't have a speck of meanness in her. She's warm, and friendly, and generous; and she always sees the best side in other people, never doubts there's something good there. She's just all-around . . . *nice.* You can't help liking her; you just can't. Even *I* can't.

Which is usually the last thing I want to be reminded of when I come back from my run, trying desperately to hang on to that wonderful, fleeting feeling of well-being . . .

Once I'm in the house I walk quickly through the kitchen, not saying hello to Dad or Terri. I ignore my reflection in the mirror opposite the kitchen countertop as I walk through to the hallway. The *last* thing I want to see after feeling so good back there on the street is my face, pudgy and red, and the way the tops of my arms are so round and . . . *flabby.*

Because that's when the questioning, the noise, starts up again in my mind: meditation time well and truly over. Tell me, *tell* me: why is it that no matter how fit I get, my body doesn't seem to look any more toned? At twenty, thirty miles a week I'd be almost as fit as the girls on the athletics team by now, surely. Yet I look—and *feel*—as wobbly as I always have.

And I'm hungrier than ever, too. I don't know what's wrong with me: all this exercise hasn't killed my appetite at all. I eat my bowl of muesli in the morning (a third of a cup of muesli, and enough milk to moisten it, but *no more;* and if no one else is in the kitchen, I thin down the milk with a little bit of water, to make it less fattening). But by ten o'clock in the morning, I'm starving. Sometimes the last lesson before lunch goes so slowly that I'm actually shaking with hunger by the time the bell goes . . .

And I feel so *guilty* for being so hungry. Whatever happened to discipline? To will? Don't I have any self-control at all?

I tell myself, over and over, that I just need to exercise more. Or to eat less, so that my stomach has the chance to shrink.

Or maybe, maybe, I just need to be less *greedy* . . .

chapter twelve

Secrets

Something strange happened this month. My period didn't come. I waited and waited, thinking it might be late. Now June has come and gone, and there hasn't been a sign of blood—not even a trickle.

Of course, they've been drumming it into us at school since Year 7 that when a girl's period stops it's one of the first symptoms of anorexia. Every year, they hand out these pamphlets in health education, which say that losing your period is a sign that you've lost too much body fat, that your body is starving. Apparently, all the calcium in your bones gets leached out; it's to do with hormones, like estrogen or something. According to the pamphlets, it can even cause osteoporosis later.

One in every hundred girls, Mrs. James, the health ed teacher, always says to us warningly. *It could be your friend next. Or YOU.*

Well, there's a girl in our class who had to go to the *hospi-*

tal last year because she was anorexic. Jessica Fuller, her name is. I remember watching her as the year went by: she came back from the Christmas holidays looking heaps slimmer than before, and then, incredibly, she just *went on* losing weight. By the middle of the year, she was so skinny you could see all the vertebrae in her spine poking out, right up to the top of her neck. Her shoulder blades stuck out through her sweater like the sharp edges of an ax, and her cheekbones were steep ridges in her face. She weighed seventy-five pounds, or something amazing like that.

And she's not the only one. There are other girls at school whose skirts hang off their hips. I mean, let's face it, it's hardly a rare disease.

So . . . so much for our wonderful health education classes. So much for all that great information they gave us about periods. None of that stopped Jessica and Co., did it?

I got my period when I was twelve. It took me completely by surprise—Nat hadn't had hers yet, and Terri, who's a year older than me, had only just started herself. And the truth is, I was too embarrassed to tell Mum. I didn't know what to say to her; I felt my body had let me down, betrayed me. In the end, I couldn't bring myself to tell anyone. I went to the supermarket and bought some pads with my pocket money and kept quiet. I tried to pretend it had never happened. Every *month,* I pretended it hadn't happened.

Then one day, when I was fifteen, Mum came into my room while I was packing my bag for a school camp. And there it was: a box of tampons sitting on the carpet beside my bag. I'll never forget the look that crossed her face: astonishment first, and then, bewilderingly, hurt.

"How've you been paying for them?" she asked at last.

I told her.

"You didn't have to do that, Lise! You *know* I pay for Terri's. They just go on the shopping list whenever she needs them."

I didn't say anything. I felt ashamed all over again—as if I'd let her down, both by having a body that did stuff when she wasn't ready for it to and, even more, for not having told her. For not having *shared* it with her.

"You should've let me know," she said, finally, getting up to leave my bedroom, the angry, hurt expression still plastered across her lipsticked face. "Did you think I'd never ask? Didn't you think I might be worried about you?"

And, of course, I *hadn't* thought of that. The idea never even entered my head. Which was yet another reason to feel ashamed of myself.

Anyway, I know it's not anorexia that's made me miss my period this month. It *can't* be; for one thing, I'm not thin enough. Besides, I read somewhere recently that there are other reasons your period can stop suddenly—like playing a lot of sports, or being under stress. What with all the running I'm doing, plus all the studying we have to do this year and the exams and stuff, I figure there are plenty of other good reasons I seem to have missed my period.

In any case, I'm far too greedy to get anorexia. Have you ever heard of an anorexic who craves food all the time?

Who thinks about it day and night? Who *never* stops feeling hungry? I don't think so.

Because I'll never forget what Jessica used to say last year if you offered her food. Even when she was really thin—even just before she went into the hospital—she'd look at you with this strange, trapped expression in her eyes. As if you were hassling her, somehow. And she'd say loudly (just as she still does now, in fact, if you offer her something like a piece of cake or a cookie), "No, thank you. I'm not hungry at the moment."

I honestly can't imagine myself ever being like that. I like eating too much. I just *do.*

On the last day of the semester, before the midyear holidays, Mr. Garvolli hands back our end-of-semester chemistry tests. He gives them out in sadistic order, from best paper to worst. I wait as he hands them back. Counting: *one, two, three . . .*

There are twenty-eight people in our class, and my test comes in tenth. I used to be in the top five of the class. Always.

And at this moment—at this moment, in front of all these people—I am the closest I've been in *years* to crying. I take a deep breath. I stare at my desk, open my eyes wide, don't let myself blink. My cheeks get hot; I can feel an ugly pink flush crawling up my neck, over my cheeks.

Don't blink, don't blink, don't blink . . .

It's not as if I don't know why I did so badly this time: the Fear came back again during the test. It took me twenty minutes to calm myself down, to be able to hold my pen firmly enough, without shaking, to write. I had half an hour left to do the test. Half an hour: that's not enough for *anyone* to do well in a test. No matter how hard they studied for it.

For several minutes, I struggle with myself. *(Don't cry. Don't CRY.)* But I win. By the time the bell rings, my eyes are dry, my cheeks normal. All under control. I even manage to smile at Sofia when she bumps into me in the locker room on her way to the cafeteria.

"Hey, Liso," she says, pushing her ponytail back over her shoulder. "What's up?"

"Nearly holidays," I say lightly. "Let's celebrate. What's for lunch? Chocolate doughnuts?" (*As if.* I can't remember the last time I had a chocolate doughnut.)

You see? Nowhere *near* tears.

Which means I'm okay for the moment; for a little while longer, at least, I'm safe. And if I can just keep following the rules—*Don't cry. Stick to your diet. Get fit. Study hard. Don't let on who you really are*—everything will be all right.

Because, I tell myself, the thing about these rules is . . . they are the things that will make other people like me. They are the things that will make me proud of myself.

They are the things that will keep me in control . . .

PART III

Nat

chapter thirteen

Alfresco's

"So what are you going to wear to the Formal?" Sofia asks me one day early in the new semester.

We're sitting in Alfresco's—Sofe, Lise, and I—enjoying the weekly Year 12 lesson-free afternoon (which is supposed to be for study purposes, but—come *on.* I don't *think* so). It's a cold, sunny afternoon, and the café is dark and deserted, the smell of hot, sweet milk mingling with stale cigarette smoke.

I don't answer Sofia's question straightaway. After a moment, I say casually—like the Year 11 and 12 Formal isn't a topic I've been absolutely dreading ever since term began—"I'm not going this year."

"Hey, nor am I," Lise chimes in, shooting a surprised, happy smile at me across the table.

Sofe ignores her. "What about Josh?" she says to me.

I shrug my shoulders.

"*Nat.* He's your *boyfriend.*"

"Yes, I know, but—"

Sofe gives me a shrewd look. "He doesn't want to go."

"No, it's not that. It's just—"

In fact, there are two reasons I don't want to go to the Formal.

The first is that after last year, I swore I'd never go to a Formal again. Last year was a *disaster.*

For starters, Sofia's boyfriend of the moment, Sebastian, got drunk and spewed up all over her dress just as they were getting out of the car to go in. She dumped him right there at the entrance to the hall and caught a taxi home by herself before she'd even gone inside. ("Mate, if I'd had another dress, believe me—I'd've put it on and caught another taxi right back again . . .")

Then there was my partner. Simon was one of Sebastian's mates, whom Sofia had had the bright idea of setting me up with two weeks before the Formal.

"You can't go by yourself," she said to me.

"Why not?" I argued. "Lise is."

"Yeah, but that's Lise," said Sofia dismissively. "Now let's go and find you a dress."

Simon was five foot three and stank of nervous sweat; and all he wanted to talk about was how he'd taken E once, and how cool it was. Also, he couldn't keep his hands off me. Even now, if I close my eyes, I can still feel the way his hands snaked up my ribs toward my breasts as we danced.

Finally, breathless and desperate to get free of him, I shouted over the music, "Let's sit down for a minute, okay?" He took me over to a bench in the darkest corner of the hall, plunked himself down next to me, and *kissed* me. His lips were all wet and rubbery, and his knee inched its way between my legs as he poked his tongue around my mouth. I thought I was going to choke—or drown—in all that anxious, eager saliva forcing its way down my throat.

As for Lise, all I can remember is her standing miserably against the wall in a sweet old-fashioned but *totally* wrong flowery cotton dress, clutching a plastic cup of lemonade. She couldn't, or wouldn't, dance. When Simon disappeared to the toilet for a brief, blissful moment, I dragged her out onto the dance floor, and she moved stiffly around for a few seconds before creeping off again at the end of the song. Then, at 10 p.m., she left the hall abruptly to call her dad to come and pick her up. I didn't see her again that evening.

So that's one reason I don't want to go to the Formal. The other is—Josh. I mean, he's *nineteen.* Do I really want to remind him how much younger (and stupider) I am than him? Besides, I just can't see him there. It's so private-schoolish. All those evening dresses, and Year 12 guys in tuxedos and bow ties, and schoolteachers handing out glasses of Coke and orange juice. It's the kind of thing Josh would have a field day with.

He hates private schools, Josh. He says they're full of rich kids, the children of elitists—and he can't *stand* elitists. Besides, he says, they push the belief that studying and being brainy are the only ways to succeed in life. "My dad belongs to Mensa. He's still totally full of himself. Look what he did to my mother."

I have a hard enough time myself trying to figure out what makes him attracted to me in the first place. I don't want *him* to start asking that question. *No way* is Sofe going to talk me into going to the Formal this year.

"Lise isn't going, either," I remind Sofia now. "You're not making a fuss about that."

"Yeah, well," she says, looking mildly bored. "Lise never goes to *anything.*"

There's a sudden, short silence. I think: *Oh, no. I wish Sofe wouldn't get started on Lise.*

"Well, she doesn't, does she?" Sofia says. She turns to Lise. "You wanna go out with me and Nat next weekend, Lise?"

Lise stares impenetrably down at her coffee—a long black—and stirs the teaspoon round and round in her cup. Eventually, she says quietly, without looking up, "I've got to study next weekend."

Sofia rolls her eyes. "See?" she says to me. "Tell me the last time she went to a party with us, or thought about going to a nightclub, or slept over, or—"

"I came out with you today," says Lise, almost inaudibly.

"To *coffee,*" says Sofia disgustedly.

"And I slept over with you both at Nat's for New Year's."

"That was six *months* ago!"

Lise traces tiny, endless patterns in her coffee cup. She's sitting with her legs crossed under the table, and her top foot swings agitatedly back and forth, nudging the plastic leg of the spare chair opposite her.

"I can't afford to go out anyway," she says, her voice still barely louder than a whisper. "I don't get much pocket money."

"Then get a job, like the rest of us!"

"But I have to study . . ."

"Oh, for God's sake, Lise," says Sofia wearily. "Just—get a *life.*"

We all shut up after this. Lise looks down, avoiding our eyes, her foot worrying away at the chair leg. Sofia sighs heavily, scrapes her chair back, stands up.

"I'm getting a gelato," she says roughly. "Anyone else want one?"

I shake my head out of loyalty to Lise, whose face, as Sofia stalks off to the counter, is tense and sucked in over her empty cup.

"Lise?" I ask carefully. "You okay?"

She takes a quick breath, doesn't look up at me. "Yeah."

"Sure?"

"I'm *fine.*"

I try to feel my way forward. "I'm sure she didn't—Sofe can be a bit—" I pause, trying to think how to put it, how to stay loyal to both of them. "You *do* know she didn't really mean it—"

Her hair swings across her face, corkscrew curls covering her eyes. "I *said,* I'm *fine.*"

I glance over at Sofe, standing at the counter by the coffee machine, talking away cheerfully to the waiter, acting like nothing ever happened, like she's forgotten the argument already. (To be fair, she probably has. Sofia never holds a grudge.) Then I look back at Lise. Her teeth are clamped down on her lip; her hand clenches her coffee cup. She looks anything but fine.

Sofe forgetting, Lise stewing. This is how it always is after one of their arguments. With me sitting in the middle of them—thinking, glaring, *wishing.*

I *hate* it when they argue. I'm just not *into* conflict resolution (sorry, Mum): I just don't want to get involved. I mean, whose side would I take? So instead I always sit there and worry about what would happen if they really got started. I'm scared of what Sofia would say to Lise, and I'm scared of the look I'd see on Lise's face—that look of silent, intractable hurt. I'm scared they'd end up never speaking to each other again.

The thing is, where would that leave *me*? They're both my friends. I want it to stay that way; I want us *all* to be friends.

chapter fourteen

Saturday night

These days, I don't call my parents on Saturday nights after work to say I'll be late home. I don't have to. They already know: Saturday night is Josh night.

Most Saturdays, we make our way down to the beach after work. Josh loves the beach—the water, the sand, the air, the sky: the wildness of it. ("Despite the litter," he always says grimly.) We walk along the sea's edge, where the sand is compact and firm, and he holds my hand, gazing out to the horizon. In the cold late-afternoon air, his cheeks get all red and—*kissable.*

When we reach his house, Josh cooks dinner for me. ("Don't you get *sick* of cooking?" I asked him once. He shook his head: "Never.") Some evenings he switches on the back-porch light while he cooks, so that while we're having dinner at his round pine table we can look through the glass sliding doors to the tiny lit-up backyard.

Other nights we sit on the sofa and listen to his music

collection. He's got weird taste in music, Josh. He likes folk music, world music, rhythm and blues; Billy Bragg, Paul Kelly, Archie Roach. But he also likes yodeling. I'm not kidding: at work he even makes Michael switch over to a station on the radio that plays yodel music for a couple of hours every Saturday afternoon.

"You've got to be happy to yodel," he said shamelessly, when I asked him about it. "I mean, *listen* to that. How could you do it if you were feeling sad?"

Yes, but. "I wouldn't call *you* the most cheerful of souls," I pointed out.

"Maybe that's why I like it," he said, shrugging.

But sometimes, now, we don't bother with dinner, or even with music. We just go straight upstairs to his bedroom. We sit on his bed, fooling around and—you know—*exploring.* Josh brushes my eyelashes with his lips and whispers "Sweet Nat" in my ear. He kisses my nose, mouth, breasts. His lips taste salty and make me think of the sea, but his breath is sweet, like the chamomile tea he drinks to help him get to sleep at night.

We kiss a lot. All over. Once we've started, it's like we can't stop kissing each other. Sometimes I have to pull myself away from him physically, saying, "Not yet, okay? Not yet." There are times, to be honest, when I don't even know why I say that. I just know that—for now—this is enough. *For now.*

But during the week, when I'm drawing diagrams in biology, or gossiping with Sofe, or lying in bed at night, drifting off to sleep, I think about Josh's room. I think about being there with him again—about being there and never leaving it. Sometimes I think his room is like a magnet—stopping me from drifting, giving me direction; drawing me on, drawing me in.

That's how I feel about Josh, too. Like I'm drawn to him and don't ever want to let go—

One evening, lying next to Josh on his bed, I notice his cloth cap (the one he wears every day at work) hanging on the hook on the back of his door.

"Where'd you get it from, that cap?" I ask idly.

"My ex."

"Julie?"

"Yeah."

Josh hasn't had a girlfriend since Julie; it had been almost a year since they broke up when he first met me. He doesn't talk about any of his old girlfriends much, but from time to time I ask him about them anyway. I kind of like it, to be honest. It adds color to him, somehow: to who he is, what he's done with his life. Also—and I know this'll sound weird—it makes him more precious to me. As in, now he's with *me.* Even though he's had other girlfriends, *I'm* the one he wants to be with now.

I still can't believe that's true.

"Is it from Thailand or somewhere?" I ask now.

"Vietnam." He sees the question in my eyes. "Julie went there at the end of the first year of our apprenticeship. For a holiday. We were going to go there together, but I couldn't afford the plane ticket."

"Was that why you two broke up?" I ask curiously. "Because she went there without you?"

He sighs. "You really want to know?"

"Well—" I hesitate. "As long as you don't mind talking about it."

He closes his eyes, rolls away from me to face the wall. "She sent me all these e-mails and postcards and letters and things while she was away, right? Something every day, pretty much." He takes a breath. "So anyway, I roll up at the airport when she gets back, all excited—you know, like, I haven't seen this girl for two whole *months*—and we drive back to my place. Then, just as we're sitting down on my bed, she tells me she 'spent a weekend' with some American dude in Vietnam." He stares at the wall. " 'Just a weekend,' she said. 'It didn't mean anything.' "

I wince. "So what did you do?"

"Broke up with her. Straightaway."

"Just like that?" I say. "No second chances?"

"You don't screw around when you're in a relationship, Nat," he says heavily. "You just *don't*."

Not unless you're Josh's dad, of course, I think grimly. Then you can "screw around" for three *years* and get away with it.

I lie there quietly next to him, propped up on my elbow, knees curled up tight into the back of his. I stare at the cap on the door, dream about buying him a new one for Christmas. He'd like that, I think. Then I say softly, "Josh?"

"Nat."

I smile, the way I always do when he says that. "Um—have you ever been to a school Formal?"

He rolls back to face me, grimaces. "No. Why?"

I hesitate. "Do you want to come to mine?"

I know, I know. I said I wasn't going to go to the Formal. I don't even know why I'm asking now, to be honest, except that suddenly I just *have* to. I shouldn't be lying to Josh about the things I do, the school I go to. He's had enough lies in his life.

Besides, I don't want to be the kind of person who shuts herself off, who's ashamed of who she is. I want to stay open. I want him to love me for being *me.*

"Do I have to wear a suit?" he asks.

I start to smile. "Yep. With a white shirt and a bow tie."

"And you'll be wearing a dress. I mean, like—a *real* one."

"Mmm-hmm. Satin, or silk, or something."

"Now that I have to see," he says, grinning.

I take that as a yes. It looks like I'm going to the Formal after all.

chapter fifteen

Blue jeans

Who ever heard of studying on a Sunday? I mean, I know we're in Year 12, but *study*? On *Sunday*?

But this is what Lise rings up to suggest one Saturday night, just as I've walked in after the tram trip home from Josh's place.

"Just for the morning, I promise," she pleads. "We can go shopping in the afternoon, if you want. I need a new sweater." She pauses, adds winningly, "I'll help you with your math while we're at it."

I groan. Since we've got a math assignment due first thing Monday morning, I can hardly refuse.

"But not before nine o'clock, okay? I need to sleep in."

I can hear the smile in her voice. "You want to come over here?"

"No, no," I say hastily. "You come over to my house. Mum and Dad are out tomorrow. We'll have the place to ourselves."

The truth is, I've never liked going over to Lise's house. All that stainless steel and wrought iron, and the mirrors—they give me the total *creeps.* Then there's Lise's sister, Terri, slinking around the house on the phone to her uni friends, looking unbelievably gorgeous. (Believe it or not, Lise told me the other day that Terri's just been offered some part-time modeling work.) Not to mention Mrs. Mawson, with her platinum-blond hair and short-short skirts and her carefully painted long red fingernails. Even listening to Tim's muffled heavy metal through my bedroom walls is better than putting up with that.

Lise arrives punctually at nine—she's never been one to be late, Lise—and we settle down in my bedroom. I offer her my desk, and spread my own books out on the floor. (My theory with homework is, if I'm not at a desk, I won't feel like I'm actually studying. Not, of course, that this has ever been known to work for me in the past.) After an hour or so, the door pushes open slightly and Magpie, our old black-and-white Border collie, wanders in, looking cold and arthritic.

"You mind if he stays?" I ask Lise.

She looks up briefly from her books, hesitates. "No, no, that's fine."

So Magpie lies down on the floor by my schoolbag, and is soon contentedly twitching and snoring in his sleep next to me.

Lise studies silently all morning, pushing her hair back over her shoulders when it spills across her face. Her concentration is ferocious: she never even yawns. Down on the floor, I crouch over my math textbook, doodling in the margins, dreaming about Josh. Already it seems *ages* since I last saw him.

Finally, at one o'clock, I jump up, walk over to Lise, and put my hands determinedly over the pages of her notebook.

"We *have* to have a break. I'm *starving.*"

Lise follows me reluctantly into the kitchen, her mind obviously still on algebraic equations.

"What d'you want for lunch?"

She hesitates. Lise never tells you what she wants to do. It's like she's scared of offending you or something.

"Sandwiches sound okay?" Not waiting for an answer, I get out bread, butter, cheese, and tomatoes, and start making myself a sandwich.

Lise watches me for a moment. "I might have a banana on mine," she says at last, taking a banana from the fruit bowl on the kitchen table. She takes a couple of pieces of bread, lays the banana in thin slices over the bread, cuts the sandwich into quarters. No butter, I notice. *Weird.*

While we're eating our sandwiches at the kitchen table, Mum comes in through the back door from the garden. She looks grumpy and tired, like she does after she's had an argument with her mother over the phone, and her eyes are pale and watery from the chilly air outside. In fact, the temperature in here isn't much warmer: our house is old and creaky, with drafts leaking from every closed window and door, and Dad refuses to put on the central heating until dinnertime. I spend the months from May through to October literally *swathed* in sweaters and scarves, huddled—like now—with my hands and my feet as close to our one ancient electric heater as possible.

Mum wanders over to us at the table, cuts off a slice of cheese for herself.

"So how's the studying going?" she asks, pulling up a chair.

I pull a face. "I can't concentrate. It's *Sunday.*"

Lise nibbles at a sandwich quarter. "I always study on Sunday."

"Hell, Lise," I say. "I can't imagine anything worse."

Besides, I think, if I did that every weekend, I wouldn't see Josh: he finishes work after lunch on Sundays. It's not just Saturday nights I spend with him now: most Sunday afternoons, I catch the tram over to his place so I can be with him for the rest of the day.

"Doesn't it make you feel guilty if you don't study?" Lise says to me.

"Guilty?" I look at her curiously. "Not really. What about you?"

"Well . . . I just want to get the best marks I can at the end of this year."

"You must really want to get into law," I say enviously. Sometimes I forget how determined Lise is: she never, ever loses sight of her goal. Once again, I find myself wishing *I* could be that determined, that sure, about something. Then I tell myself: Well, there *is* something I'm sure about these days—*Josh.*

But Lise puts her half-eaten sandwich down and says,

frowning, "It's not that I want to get into law so much. It's just—I feel so *guilty* when I don't study."

"How much *are* you studying, exactly, Lise?" Mum asks sharply.

I groan inwardly. Here we go: another deep Mum-and-Lise conversation.

But Lise pushes her plate away, avoiding my mother's eyes. "Not enough. Not *nearly* enough."

Mum pushes on, determined. "You've always studied hard, my dear. You don't want to overdo it."

"No, no . . . ," says Lise.

"Because there *is* such a thing as *too much* studying, you know."

"Mum—" I start to say.

She ignores me. "Try not to feel so guilty, Lise. All you can do is your best, you know. You can't do more than that."

"Mum!"

"What?"

I can't *stand* it when my mother gets all heavy on my friends. I mean, did we even invite her to sit down with us?

"Can't you just— We were just trying to— Listen, we're going shopping."

She's right about one thing, though, I think as I jump up. That word "guilty": Lise has used it twice in the last five minutes. She says it like no one else says it—strong, and heavy, and emphatic. Like it's a *sin,* almost.

I shove our plates in the sink. Lise stays at the table, watching me. She looks as cold as I feel: like me, she's shivering, and there are goose pimples on her wrists. She's holding her hands so close to the heater she's almost touching it.

"Come on," I say, hoisting her up from her seat. "I can't stand talking about studying anymore. It's so depressing. Let's go."

Magpie pads out after us, leaving Mum alone in the kitchen. He stands at the back door, watching us go with big, dark, reproachful dog eyes.

We spend *hours* searching for the right sweater for Lise. You'd think it wouldn't be that hard, given that she only ever wears black tops. (Unlike Sofia, who wears every style of clothing under the sun as long as it's brightly colored, Lise always wears the same thing: jeans and a black top. I'm serious: the only thing that changes is that in summer it's a black T-shirt and in winter it's a black sweater.)

But it's an exhausting process. Every time Lise tries something on, she stares at herself in the mirror, picking nervously at it, saying, "It just doesn't *sit* right." She smoothes the top down again over her chest, bites her lip. No matter how many times I say, "That looks great!" she just looks more and more anxious.

Finally, in desperation, I pick out a pair of jeans for myself in what feels like the hundredth store we have been in. I try them on.

"Here," I say, taking them off and handing them to her over the cubicle wall. "Try these on instead." I mean, maybe she'll be less fussy about jeans than she is about tops. You never know—it's worth a try.

"They'd be too tight for me," says Lise.

I sigh. "You're a size 12, too, aren't you? They fit *me* okay. I'd buy them for myself if I had any money left in my bank account."

I stand outside her dressing room, waiting impatiently.

"You should come to the Formal this year, Lise. Just—you know—have fun this time and not worry about anything else."

"*Nat.* I don't *want* to."

I sigh. "Why not?"

"What's the point?" she says quietly, through the cubicle wall. "I hate dancing; you know I do. And it's not as if I've got a partner to take with me. You've got Josh now. It's *different.*"

This is the only time Lise has ever mentioned Josh by name to me. Ever since I've been going out with him—and that's *months* now—she's never once asked anything about him. I stopped bringing his name up with her long ago. What's the point? She just doesn't want to know about him.

But she doesn't say anything more about Josh now. Instead, she opens the cubicle door to show me the jeans.

"They're too big," she says, puzzled.

At first I don't believe her. She's been fussing around all afternoon about how nothing fits—*yeah, yeah, so what's new?* Then I inspect her more closely. She's right: the jeans literally sag at her waist. You could fit a hand comfortably between her stomach and the beltline, and her butt looks almost nonexistent inside all that extra denim.

"Wow," I say enviously. "You've lost weight."

She looks at me, marveling. "They *are* pretty loose. Must be all the running."

I still can't quite believe what I'm seeing. The jeans are at least *two* sizes too big.

"You want to try on a size 8?" I ask slowly.

Lise just laughs and shakes her head. "I haven't lost *that* much weight, Nat."

But she has. Oh, yes, she *has.*

Outside, the wind's rushing through Rundle Mall.

"Let's go and have an ice cream to celebrate," I suggest. "I mean, hey—you're skinny now. You can eat all the ice cream you like."

Eating ice cream in cold weather is a kind of tradition with Lise and me. She told me once, years ago, that she reckoned it actually tasted better in cold weather than in hot: "It lasts longer. And it doesn't melt all over you."

Now, though, she shakes her head at my suggestion, and a funny expression crosses her face.

"Ice cream has *dairy* products in it."

"So?"

Lise pulls her jacket tighter around her chest in the cold winter wind.

"I've decided to go vegan," she says calmly.

I listen to this in utter disbelief. "Since when?"

"I've been reading all these articles about veganism recently," she tells me, and then adds brightly, "It's the next logical step in vegetarianism, really, isn't it? If you truly believe in preventing cruelty to animals."

This is sounding less and less like the Lise I know. She's breaking all the rules: we agreed to go vegetarian, not vegan. Lise *never* breaks rules.

"How about a soyaccino, then?" I say quickly. "Or an herbal tea, or—I don't know—something equally repulsive—" I can hear the sudden desperation in my voice.

But Lise shakes her head again. "Let's skip it, okay? If we run, we could make the five o'clock bus."

I follow her wordlessly down the brick-paved mall. She walks briskly, looking straight ahead, arms folded to keep in the warmth; her fingertips, sticking out from underneath her arms, are purple. She's wearing a *belt,* I realize suddenly. It's buckled in around her old jeans—the ones she bought at the beginning of last year. Back then, those jeans were too tight.

"Slender" is not a word I would ever have used to describe Lise before—curvy, yes; big-hipped; *chunky,* even. But she didn't look like any of those things back in the shop. I mean, don't get me wrong—there are definitely girls at school who are skinnier than her. (You know, those lucky girls who eat doughnuts and chips all day and *still* manage to look like they've just come off a catwalk.)

It's just—she's shrunk, somehow. She looks so much smaller than she used to. So much more *fragile.*

"Did you get the sweater?" Mum asks me later, over dinner.

She looks grumpy again, like she did at lunch: she's definitely rung her mother today. Mum—unlike her two older sisters—doesn't get on with Gran; she never has. Dad's theory is that that's why she was so happy to move to another state with him when they met, despite the fact that she missed the rest of her family. Still, she calls Melbourne faithfully once a week, and she and Gran have these long, painful conversations that you can hear from one end of the house to the other.

"Mum," you'll hear my mother say, a few minutes into the phone conversation, "you *know* I can't move back to Melbourne."

She'll pause. Then, a moment later, her voice rising: "Of course I'll come and visit again soon—"

Pause.

"That's not true. I come and visit three times a year, *every* year, without *fail*—"

A long silence here.

"Of *course* I care about you—"

Silence again. By now she's pacing the length of the phone cord, Mum, her face twisted with anger.

"You're *not* a frail old lady. *Don't* play those games with me now. I said, don't play *games* with me—"

It's the same argument every week. They never resolve it; they never move on; and they never, ever call it quits between each other. So much for conflict resolution, Mum.

The worst thing is when Mum hangs up on Gran. Afterward, she marches into her bedroom, pulls on her track pants, yells out, "I'm going for a run." It's the only time she ever exercises: she's not supposed to anymore, because of her bad knees. But no one ever stops her from going. I think we'd rather she *crippled* herself than sat around fuming about Gran.

Now I nod in answer to her question.

"Guess what color sweaters Lise tried on today?"

She grins. "Hmm . . . Let me think. Could it have been black?"

Tim reaches past Dad across the table and helps himself to another roast potato. (It's actually kind of weird having Tim here for dinner: he's just started going out with some girl he met through a mate at work, and he hardly ever comes home. Not even to sleep.)

"She's weird, your friend Lisa," he says.

"Lise," I say crossly. "Not Lisa. *Lise.*"

"Whatever. She *is.* Does she ever actually speak?"

"Not around you. I mean, who *would?*"

"She's looking very fit and toned these days," Mum remarks.

I glare at her. "What d'you mean?"

"I thought perhaps she'd gone on a bit of a diet, that's all," she says mildly. "You know—lost all that 'puppy fat' Jen Mawson's always scolding her for."

Mum doesn't like Lise's mother. It's not surprising, I suppose: they're total opposites. Not that I blame her, to be honest: I don't like Lise's mother much, either.

"She's just getting fit," I say defensively. "She's taken up running. You know—that thing *you're* not supposed to do?"

But unluckily for me, Mum fails to rise to the bait. She

rests her elbow on the table, fork in her other hand. She's got that annoying, concerned, *mulling* look on her face.

"So you don't think she's deliberately trying to lose weight, then, Nat?"

"Not that I know of," I snap.

Shut up, I'm thinking. *Shut up, shut up, shut UP.* It drives me crazy the way my mother interferes. Lise is *my* friend: *I'm* the one who's supposed to know what's going on in her head. Besides, what about me? What about what's going on in *my* life?

So I don't tell her about the bus trip home today with Lise.

We didn't say anything to each other after she refused the ice cream. In the bus, we sat facing each other, not talking. Lise stared out the window intently. I sighed and shifted uncomfortably opposite her, trying to catch her eye. They say that's the sign of true friendship, don't they?—that you can sit comfortably with someone and not say anything at all. But I wasn't comfortable. I've never felt like that with Lise before. It was like I was sitting with a *stranger.*

Just before the bus reached her stop, Lise stood up, pushing her arms through the straps of her backpack with a grimace.

"See you, Nat."

"Yeah. See ya."

She squeezed her way down the aisle, pushed the door open, climbed off the bus. Through the window I saw her stop by a nearby telephone pole to tug at her sweater, pull it back down underneath her backpack. She trudged around the corner as the bus pulled away, head down, not looking back at me, not waving.

All I could think, all the way home from there, was: Something is wrong. Lise, Lise, I *know* something is wrong—

chapter sixteen

Rainy afternoon

"You want to go out on the porch?"

I come and join Josh at the sliding door.

"It looks a bit *cold,*" I say doubtfully.

He picks up my hand, threads his fingers through mine. "You big wuss."

It's a Sunday afternoon—dark, blustery, the rain sleeting in at the windows. I shouldn't even be here, to be honest: I should be refusing all invitations at this stage and staying home to study. (Yes, I admit—even I am succumbing to the panic-study bug now: I'm getting so behind with my schoolwork, it's not *funny.*) But when Josh rang in the morning as usual and invited me over, I just said *yes.* I couldn't say no, that's the thing; I just couldn't resist him. I can't *ever* resist Josh.

Today he's been teasing me, trying to find out about the dress I've bought for the Formal, which is next weekend. I told him it was going to be a surprise. Now, standing at the porch door with me, he tries again.

"Let me guess. It's black and slinky."

I shake my head.

"Green. Velvet."

I smile. *No.*

"All right, then. It's a big, swirly gold number, with *sequins.*"

"*Josh!*" The idea of me in sequins is too revolting to contemplate, and I give in at last. "As a matter of fact, it's pink."

He raises an eyebrow. "What, like—shocking pink?"

"*Pale* pink, thank you very much."

He looks at me, considering. "*Baby* pink." Then he sees my face, says hastily, "I mean—I didn't mean—"

"What *did* you mean?" I ask pointedly.

"You'll look great, Nat," he says quickly. "I know you will. *Whatever* you wear."

He wanders over to the stereo to put some music on, comes back to me, opens the sliding door. We stand in the doorway, looking out onto the porch, feeling the wind brush against our cheeks. I hum to the music, singing the lyrics under my breath.

"You've been hanging around me too long," he says, wrapping his arms around my waist and pressing his knees into the backs of my thighs, maneuvering me out onto the porch. "You know the words to all my albums."

We sit down on the wooden decking, our backs against the brick wall of the house. There's a native creeper twined around the porch posts; its leaves flap wildly in the wind. I snuggle into Josh, trying to stay warm.

"So, what's the latest on *Home and Away*?" he asks.

This is one of our regular conversations. I fill him in on the last week's happenings.

"*Must* get a TV one of these days," he says sarcastically when I've finished.

Josh thinks TV is evil. Literally, like—*evil*. It saps your creativity, he says; it's just a huge marketing exercise. It programs you into thinking the way "they" want you to think. Sometimes I can see what he means—just like I can see what he means about the problem with McDonald's and KFC. But I never tell him this. I like watching *Home and Away* too much.

"So anyway," I say, "I think they're going to get back together again in a couple of weeks. You can see it a *mile* off."

Josh moves closer into me, not answering. He puts his hand on my thigh, just resting it there, and I can feel the weight of him through his hand, his warmth. It makes my skin tingle.

"You wearing perfume?" he asks me.

"Yeah. D'you like it? It's called Rainforest."

He buries his head in my neck. "You smell wonderful."

Soon we are kissing—slowly, but with this sweet, tugging warmth growing between us. Josh's hands are everywhere, and everywhere he touches me, I grow warmer. This is the Josh I think about at night in bed, or when I close my eyes at school and daydream: his skin, his breath, the brush of his hair across my face, his hand on my breast.

I pull back, suddenly shaky. "I should go. I've got *masses* of homework."

The faintest look of irritation washes across his face and then is gone. He smiles. "Right now? You sure?"

I hesitate. "Walk me to the tram stop?"

The thing is, I'm *not* sure—not at all. Things have changed: kissing's not enough anymore, even for me. *Soon,* I tell him silently. I promise it to myself, too: *Soon, soon . . .*

chapter seventeen

Health kick

One lunchtime Sofia and I sit in the rec room, gossiping. It's a Thursday, so it's just the two of us: Lise has choir on Thursday at lunchtime.

"It's Lise's birthday soon," I say.

"I know. The day after the Formal."

I'm surprised. Sofia's usually hopeless with dates.

"Is she doing anything this year?"

I sigh. "She *says* she doesn't want to. She *says* she's got too much studying."

Sofe rolls her eyes. "I would never have guessed."

"I was thinking we could have a breakfast party for her."

"You mean like a surprise one?"

I shake my head violently, appalled at the thought.

"Lise *hates* surprise parties. I just thought—something small, you know? You, me, and Lise, at my house or something. On the morning after the Formal. We could each bring something to eat."

"Sounds nice," says Sofia absently.

We're sitting on the big, wide windowsill on the far side of the room. I lean with my back against the glass, looking out over the rest of the room, which is full of other Year 12s eating lunch. Sofe has one leg tucked underneath her on the sill, facing side-on to me, peering out through the window across the yard, toward the library.

"She's vegan now, you know."

Sofia pulls her other leg up to her chin, pulling her skirt down over her knee as she does so. "Who?"

"Lise."

"Since when?"

"She told me the other day," I say, shrugging. "She said it was the *next logical step.*"

I expect her to groan and roll her eyes, in typical Sofia style, but she doesn't. She gazes out the window thoughtfully.

"Well, she's got a point."

"Yes, I know, but—"

She turns back to me. "But what?"

I hesitate. I don't know how to say what I want to say. The thing is, despite what I said to Mum the other day, I can't get rid of that picture of Lise, standing there in Rundle Mall, shivering with cold, saying, "Those size 12 jeans would be too tight for me." I keep seeing the expression on her face when I suggested we have an ice cream: that look of panic, of guilt, of *fear.* It reminds me of Jessica Fuller—popular, pretty Jessica Fuller, darling of the trendy "in" set—who got anorexic last year and spent all her lunchtime pacing manically up and down the schoolyard, with her stockings falling in looser and looser wrinkles around her legs. All she ever said was, "I wish I was *really* skinny." She looked so ugly. So *sick*.

Is that what's going to happen to Lise?

"Sofe," I say carefully, "d'you think Lise is all right?"

Sofia looks puzzled. She shifts uncomfortably on the sill. "What d'you mean?"

"Well, like—have you noticed how much *weight* she's lost this year?"

"Yes," she says immediately. "She looks really good."

"I s'pose—"

"Don't you think? She's always gone on about how fat she is. And she's never exactly been fit, has she? Good for her, I reckon. We could *all* probably use a bit of exercise."

"Yeah," I say, unconvinced.

A look of impatience crosses her face.

"What're you trying to *say,* Nat?"

"I just—Lise *worries* me sometimes, you know? I keep thinking—"

But I can't bring myself to say the actual word. I mean, maybe I'm wrong about the whole thing. It's like tempting fate: if I say it out loud, I might make it happen.

"It's just a health kick," says Sofia. "That's all it is. She won't stick to it. No one ever does."

"Yeah," I say again. "Maybe you're right."

"I'd *better* be right," Sofia says darkly.

In the background, the school bell rings, its shrill electric tone dulled by the babble of lunchtime voices. Sofia unfolds herself from the windowsill, stretches backwards from her hips, her arms above her head.

"So what're you going to make for Lise's birthday?"

I stand up with her. "Well, I *had* thought of baking a chocolate cake—"

"Yum."

"But she doesn't eat that stuff anymore!" I wail. "She's *vegan*."

We make our way out of the rec room into the passageway. When we reach the stairs, Sofia stops suddenly and leans against the handrail, pondering. Then she says slowly, "I've got the *best* vegan chocolate cake recipe at home. I found it on the Net. D'you want me to get you a copy?"

"Vegan chocolate cake?" I say doubtfully.

She laughs at the expression on my face. "No, for real—it's delicious. Lise'll *love* it."

"You reckon?"

"I promise. You'll have her totally *begging* for more."

I mean, what can I say? If I can find a recipe that makes Lise eat second helpings—that'll prove to me that I'm wrong about her—I'll try it. *Whatever* it is.

chapter eighteen

Formal

"Smile!" says the photographer.

We're standing in a booth in the foyer, Josh and I, outside the main hall. Behind us, a queue of people has formed; everyone wants to have a photo they can stick in their album and write *Year 12 Formal* underneath. I put my head on Josh's chest and beam from ear to ear at the camera. There's a flash, and then the photographer says, "All over now. You can pick the photo up at the end of the night."

We stumble out of the booth into the main hall. There are glittering silver balls hanging from the ceiling, colored crepe streamers, balloons, flashing lights. The music is loud—surprisingly loud; *satisfyingly* loud—and the dance floor is already crowded. The dancers, swishing and swaying in their silk dresses and sleek tops and tails, look like gorgeous, exotic, alien fish.

Josh and I turn back to each other. I take his hand.

"You look so *cute* in pink," he whispers into my ear.

"You don't look bad yourself," I say.

In fact, he looks so stunning he makes my stomach drop. His blond hair falls in a short, thick curtain over his forehead and his legs are a mile long in his black trousers. I can even see his muscles ripple faintly through his white shirt. (He's been cycling and training really hard recently, and it *shows.*) The two dimples swim up and down his face when he smiles, like tadpoles.

"Come on," I say quickly. "Let's dance!"

Colored lights wash over our skin. The music pours through us, bathing everyone in a humming, pulsing throb. We swim through the crowd, out onto the dance floor.

Coming off the dance floor to get our breath back some time later, we catch sight of Sofia and Nick over at the drink table. Sofia waves.

I tug Josh's hand. "You want to go over and say hello?"

Josh smiles down at me. There's sweat on his forehead, and his hair is damp. He's every bit as good a dancer as I'd hoped.

"For sure. Anyway, I'd *kill* for a drink."

"Of lemonade, naturally." Every year, the drink table is patrolled by the ever-vigilant members of the Volunteer Parents Formal Committee: it's strictly soft drinks and orange juice only.

The dimples bob around his mouth again as he follows me across the dance floor. "What else?"

Sofia's wearing a purple silky-looking dress, low-waisted and narrow in a kind of 1920s style.

"Found it in a thrift store," she tells me, beaming. "For twenty bucks!"

Nick, looking unusually clean-cut (as in, there are no loose hairs straggling out of his ponytail or falling over his face, and he's even shaved), exchanges pleasantries with Josh about football while Sofe and I talk.

"How do they *do* that?" Sofia complains to me. "Two intelligent guys—wouldn't dream of mentioning the word 'pigskin' to either of us, hey. But get them together in the same room for a couple of minutes and you'd think they never talked about anything else."

"Part of their genetic makeup," I say sardonically. "Along with facial hair and biceps."

She rolls her eyes. "And a *total* lack of brains."

The plan is for us all to leave together, dropping Josh off on the way; I'm to stay the night at Sofe's. Nick's driving, supposedly so he can drop Sofia and me off and then go on home himself. Realistically, though, I know I'll end up being shunted into the spare room so he can sleep with Sofe.

As we talk, Josh's arm snakes around my waist. I move closer into him, feeling his skin through his shirt.

"You want to dance some more, Josh?"

He groans, more for the benefit of Nick, I suspect, than from any deep-seated unwillingness to dance.

"Already?" Then he pinches my cheek affectionately. "Come on, then."

I wave at Sofia as we push our way back onto the dance floor.

* * *

Toward the end of the evening, the dancing between the two of us changes. Josh notices it, too: I can feel the sudden, smooth flowing of his movements with mine, the way his breath, like mine, is growing heavier. It feels as if we're not dancing at all—like we're connected to each other, somehow; like I'm giving myself to him, limb by limb. Everything swells; the music rolls through us like a warm, drumming wave.

"Come back home with me," he whispers into my ear.

"I can't," I protest, weakly. "You know I can't. Nick's giving us a lift."

"He's dropping me off on the way. You could just get out with me."

"But I promised my parents—"

His lips brush against my hair, my eyelids, my lips. "Sofia'll cover for you."

Laughter—weird, happy, excited laughter—surges up my throat.

"You don't *really* want to stay at Sofe's." His finger moves across my lips, and his arm passes lightly—accidentally?—across my breasts. "Nat?"

He's right, of course. Sofia *will* cover for me.

We sit side by side on the edge of his bed in our Formal clothes, like a brother and sister in fancy dress.

"Are you nervous?" Josh asks.

I nod. "A bit."

"So'm I," he says softly.

"But it's not the same for you!" I protest. "You've done this before."

He nibbles my ear. "Not with you."

It's not that I'm nervous, exactly, even though—I'll admit it—I'm trembling all over. It's that I'm scared of being disappointed, you know? This is something I want so, so much.

"Josh?" I murmur, as he unzips my dress.

"—Nat."

"—I love you—"

His kisses chase around my neck, down my stomach. The words wash out of me from some faraway shore.

"I do. I love you."

His fingers stumble only once—on the bra strap. *There's something about men and bra straps,* I remember hearing someone—Sofia? my mother, after a few glasses of white wine?—say once. *They're incompatible. Too much for the male IQ.* So I push Josh's fingers gently away and undo the clasp myself.

Josh smiles. He doesn't stumble again.

People say the first time—for a girl, anyway—is never any good. Mum told me this when she gave me her "Facts of Life, Part Five" spiel. ("Sex is like anything else in life, Nat. It's a learning process.") Even Sofia agrees on this one. "My first time was *crap.* Mate, I thought: *Never again.*")

Well, people are wrong. For me, anyway.

There are some things you can't describe, I suppose. Josh is gentle, and he jokes to put me at ease. I can see the shadow of his ribs rising underneath his brown, freckled skin, and he bathes me in his brown, laughing eyes. I feel a wave rise and sink inside of me.

And all the time, he says my name, over and over again: "Nat, Nat, sweet Nat—"

chapter nineteen

Chocolate cake

Sofia arrives at my house first, the handle of a big wicker basket over one arm.

"Lamingtons!" I say, peering inside the basket. "And *fairy bread*. Yum."

She smiles. "You gotta have fairy bread at a birthday party."

A moment later, we're letting Lise in through the back door. She's wearing a big, baggy Windbreaker and running shoes, her hair scraped back into a messy half bun.

"Sorry I'm late," she says. "I went for a run before I came here."

Next to me, I see Sofe, her eyes skipping over Lise with sudden alertness: in her track pants, Lise looks pale, tired, impossibly slender. She thrusts a glass bowl at me as she follows me into the kitchen.

"I made some fruit salad to go with the other stuff. Thought we should at least have *something* healthy."

"What—no soy milk yogurt?" says Sofia sarcastically.

We lay the food out on the kitchen table.

"Mum and Dad're out," I tell the two of them. "Went for a Sunday walk. So we've got the house to ourselves."

I rummage around in the kitchen drawers for a box of matches, light the candles I stuck into the cake earlier this morning. Then Sofia and I sing a tuneless version of "Happy Birthday" while Lise blushes and stares at the ground: "You didn't have to *do* this, guys."

After we've finished singing, she blows the candles out obediently and takes the knife I hand her. I hold my breath, waiting to see what she will do. Without looking up at us, she cuts three big hunks of cake, all the same size. I let my breath out in relief. Maybe Sofia was right, I think; maybe everything's going to be all right after all.

"It looks delicious," Lise says enthusiastically.

"And the amazing thing is, it's totally vegan," I say quickly, just in case she hasn't heard me say this the last three times.

Lise doesn't answer. She grabs a teaspoon and scoops several spoonfuls of fruit salad onto her plate, on top of the piece of cake. Then, while Sofia and I pig out on chocolate cake and lamingtons, she eats her fruit salad, teaspoon by infinitesimal teaspoon, three bites to each spoon.

Sofia eyes Lise's strange new eating habits skeptically.

"It's a fantastic cake," she says to me after a moment, deliberately.

"Thanks," I say nervously. "You'd never know it has no eggs."

The thing is, it *is* delicious. Despite the fact that I'd never have made it if I hadn't been so worried about Lise, it's actually the best chocolate cake I've ever made. It's moist and chocolaty and dark. I reckon even Josh'd be proud of this effort.

Finally, by the time Sofia's moved on to the fairy bread and I'm eating my second piece of cake, Lise finishes her fruit salad. She puts her spoon down on her plate, stretches.

"*God,* I'm full," she says, yawning luxuriously. "That was delicious. Thank you both *so* much."

She reaches for her mug of black coffee. Wrapping her hands around it, she brings it to her face, resting her cheek against its warmth. Sofia and I exchange glances over the lamingtons and fairy bread. Lise's slice of cake—the one she cut for herself, exactly the same as ours—sits in front of her, untouched on her plate.

There is a moment's silence.

"Eat your cake, Lise," Sofia says abruptly.

Lise puts her mug down, startled; her eyes go strangely wary. She looks almost trapped. My stomach clenches with sudden foreboding.

"I'd love to," she says. "It's just—I had so much fruit salad. I couldn't eat another mouthful."

Sofia leans across the table, pushes Lise's plate back toward her.

"It's a present. Nat *made* it for you."

"I know—"

"It's *rude* to refuse presents."

"I'm *not,*" Lise says quickly. "I'll eat some later."

Sofia's eyes don't waver from Lise's face.

"You are *so* full of it," she says evenly. "We all *know* you won't eat it later. You'll throw it in the bin, or feed it to the cat, or—"

"Lise doesn't have a cat," I protest weakly, breaking in. I'm trying to divert her, stem her attack. *I don't want this argument to happen.*

But Sofia ignores me.

"If you want to lose weight—which, by the way, you don't need to do—why don't you take up some kind of sport?" she says to Lise. Her tone is belligerent.

"I do. I *have.*" Lise takes a quick, shaky breath. "I run."

Sofia rolls her eyes. "I mean, like tennis. Or hockey. Or basketball. A team sport."

"But I'm no *good* at team sports—"

"Yeah, yeah, I know," Sofia says heavily. "You're no good at *anything.* How could we forget?"

My breath catches. Lise falls suddenly, heartrendingly silent. She stares at the plate of cake in front of her, her forehead knotted.

"Lighten *up,* mate," says Sofia simply. "Just *lighten up.*"

Everything goes quiet then. Here we are again, I think: Sofia haranguing, Lise hurting, me wishing they'd both just *stop.*

But then Lise lifts her head. The look on her face is unbearable, like she's—*stricken.* It's the look I've always dreaded, the look I've always hoped we'd avoid.

"I don't mind about the cake," I say quickly, stupidly, into the silence.

They both swing their eyes to me, uncomprehendingly.

"Lise?" I speak quietly, looking only at her. "I *don't* mind. Honestly."

She doesn't answer.

I stumble on, urgent, clumsy in my need to smooth things out. My words fall over each other.

"All Sofe means is, she's worried about you. You've lost *heaps* of weight. And it's great—don't get me wrong; we both think you look great. It's just—you don't want to get *too* thin—"

She's breathing easier now. I can see the muscle in her jaw relaxing as I speak.

"I'm okay," she says to me. "I'll be fine. I'm just a bit tired."

Suddenly we're talking to each other like there's no one else in the room. Our voices are soft, secretive.

"I know. We're *all* tired."

"It's Year 12."

"It's the pits."

"I get so *stressed* about it sometimes—"

"Tell me about it."

Sofia moves her head back and forth between Lise and me. She seems puzzled, like she thinks we're speaking some other language that she doesn't understand. Like she's missed what's going on between us, and she knows she's missed it, but she can't grasp why.

"We didn't mean to hassle you," I go on to Lise.

"It's okay."

"I mean, it's good to eat healthily—"

"Nat," says Sofia sharply.

I stop. "What?"

She looks at me hard, as if she's about to say something. Then she changes her mind, shrugs.

"Oh, well. Have it your way." She turns to Lise. "It's your life, anyway."

Then Lise does the strangest thing. She turns to Sofia and she *smiles.* It's a weird smile: not forgiving or understanding; not apologetic, even. It's full of secrets, this smile.

"Yes," she says quietly. "It is."

Over the last couple of months, people at school have been giving Lise quite a lot of praise about the way she looks.

In a way, I can see why. In her school uniform, she's lithe and slender; she has no ugly bulges or swellings like the rest of us. Sometimes I even feel a bit jealous of her: I wish *I* could be disciplined enough to get up early every morning and go jogging before school.

Recently, though, the compliments have changed slightly. Now, when people notice her, they say, "How come you're so *skinny*?" There's still a hint of envy in their voices, of course (that puzzled, hushed envy that everyone uses on skinny people, you know?), because although Lise must be the thinnest girl in our class by now, she's not what you'd call bony. Anyway, fragile is—you know—*trendy.*

But if you listen carefully, there's another question in

their voices—one that they're just too polite, or too scared, to ask out loud. It's *Has she got what I think she's got?*

Sofe didn't ask, though. She *said* it, loud and clear: *I KNOW you've got it.*

Sometimes I hate the way Sofia does that—says the things other people don't say; the things they can't say, *won't* say.

It takes guts, that's what I can't stand—the kind of guts I just don't have.

chapter twenty

Julie

We lie side by side on the bed, Josh's leg crossed over mine, my head tucked into his neck. Next to me, on the bedside table, are a packet of condoms (opened) and the photo from the Formal last week. I don't think I've ever smiled so widely for the camera before.

It's six o'clock in the evening. Josh, the eternal insomniac, yawns.

"Sorry," he says—and then yawns again. "I didn't get to sleep until 3 a.m. last night. I'm *so* tired."

"You'd have slept okay if *I'd* been here," I say, digging my elbow into his ribs.

He smiles. "Stay for dinner?"

But I can't; I just can't. Homework's absolutely screaming at me. The exams are less than two months away now, and I'm *way* behind. It's just that I've been too happy in the last few months to do anything about it. Being with Josh makes me feel so good.

It's weird—whenever I'm away from Josh now, my thoughts rush back to Lise: wondering what I can do, who I can talk to, who could *do* something about her. But the moment I'm back with him, my head fills up with him, only him, and I forget all my worries about Lise. There's just no *room* for anyone else in my head when Josh is around.

Right now he's shaking his head at me in mock disapproval. "Planning to cram for the exams, are we?"

"It's the only way I'll ever get through them now!" I wail.

But even so, I make no effort to get up. Without even trying, he's tugging at me, drawing me in; I still can't break his pull.

Josh half stifles another yawn, oblivious of all this. He folds his arms underneath his head.

"Might go for a hill ride tomorrow."

"Lucky you," I say sarcastically.

"Gotta do it, Nat. It's part of my training." Then he grins and pokes me back in the ribs, exactly where I poked him a couple of minutes ago. "Anyway, admit it. You'd rather study than go for a hard ride any day—wouldn't you, now?"

I don't even bother to answer this: by now, my exercise laziness is legendary between the two of us. Instead, for about the millionth time, I lie there admiring him for his dedication. He's never once given up on his dream of riding to Perth, Josh; he's been training so long now, and so hard, it seems to have become almost second nature to him.

It makes me feel left out, sometimes, to be honest—this long-term, high-flung dream of his. It's like he has a secret side to himself: a side he won't share with me, that's all his. I keep thinking: *Where do I fit into all of this?* The answer always comes back to me: *I don't.*

But does that matter? Do I have to fit into *everything* in his life? I don't know. I don't want to think about it, to analyze it; I just want to enjoy what I have.

Besides, recently I've been dreaming up plans of my own. Instead of saving up to get a car this summer, I've decided to buy myself a plane ticket to Perth. I want to, like—*be* there to greet him at the finishing line.

I haven't told Josh about my idea yet. I'm sure he'd like it, but this is *my* secret. I want it to be a surprise for him.

Through the open window, the smell of barbecued chops wafts in on the breeze. My thoughts drift longingly away from plane tickets to white bread, tomato sauce, burned sausages. I know this is the first year I've ever managed to keep my New Year's resolution for so long—but right now, I'd give anything to break it. Broccoli just isn't the same.

Josh shifts slightly on the bed, breaking my reverie.

"I bumped into Julie the other day," he says, hands behind his head, staring up at the ceiling.

My breath catches. Julie, Josh's ex—the heartbreaker in Vietnam.

" 'Bumped into' her?"

"Yeah. She was at the beach." He closes his eyes, like he's not going to say anything more about it.

I stare at the cloth cap hanging off the hook on his door. Finally, I say, "How long's it been since you last saw her?"

He shrugs. "Not since we broke up. She never spoke to me again."

There's a short silence between us.

"She told me she's started cycling again," he says after a moment, conversationally. "Remember how I told you she was into fitness in a big way? She suggested we go riding together sometime." He glances sideways at me on the bed.

I lie still, trying to relax my shoulders.

"As *friends,* Nat."

"Yeah. I know." I breathe slowly, in and out, getting my thoughts together. "Okay."

I lie there next to him, not speaking. Mum has always said that jealousy is a pointless emotion. If you love someone, she says, your love for them—like your trust—comes free of strings. Free of "ifs" and "buts."

Yeah, but she's a social worker, I think now, sardonically. *What would SHE know?*

In the end, I can't help myself. "Josh?"

"Nat."

"This doesn't change anything between us, does it?"

"Of course not. Does it for *you*?"

I hesitate. "No."

The cloth cap stares malevolently back at me from the door. I take another deep breath.

"Are you *sure* it doesn't change anything?"

He sighs, rolls over onto his side, kisses me. His lips are soft on my skin, and our kisses wander over each other.

"Sweet Nat," he whispers into my ear.

PART IV

Lise

chapter twenty-one

Hungry girl

The exams are so close now, you can almost smell them. Every time I open my books to study, a hot, sick wave rushes over me. *I'm going to fail.*

The Fear comes almost every day now. It hits at any time: not just during tests and exams, and not just at school, either; some nights, it even stops me from getting to sleep. Generally, it only lasts for a few minutes—perhaps half an hour, at most—but it *feels* much longer than that.

Sometimes, if it comes on in the middle of a lesson, I blank out completely. I sit there, covered in sweat, knees trembling uncontrollably underneath my table. I swallow huge gulps of air, stare down at my books so no one can guess what's going on. And I say, over and over again inside my head, as if it's some kind of private mantra, *Please let this go away. Please let this go away. Please let it go away . . .*

I don't understand. It's not as if there's any good reason for me to feel this way: my life is totally secure and comfortable—privileged, in fact. My parents are still together; they have plenty of money, and they love me. And I don't have any sicko uncles or cousins who raped me when I was a kid. Why am I making such a *fuss* about everything?

But no one else I know seems to experience this kind of feeling. What is the *matter* with me?

One Monday morning, in the lesson before lunch, the Fear lasts the whole lesson. By the end, as the last of the sickness ebbs away, I am exhausted. My hair clings in damp tendrils to my forehead, and the aftershocks still tremble all the way through me. It's all I can do to stand up and make it to the classroom door.

Nat comes over to me as I stumble toward my locker.

"You look exhausted, Lise," she says gently. "Are you okay?"

She's been asking me this a lot recently. I don't like it. It makes me wonder what she knows about me. And it confuses me, too: one moment she's all sweet and caring; the next she's laughing with Sofia over some secret joke about their boyfriends. It seems ages since Nat and I laughed together about something.

"I'm just tired," I say, truthfully enough. "I didn't sleep very well the last couple of nights."

Immediately she's concerned. "Why don't you go to the infirmary? Have a bit of a lie-down?"

I shake my head. "I'll be all right. I just need to go outside for a moment and get some fresh air."

She opens her mouth, and I can see her words coming before she says them: *I'll go with you.* But I'm still cloaked in the aftermath exhaustion of the Fear, and desperate to be alone.

"I'll catch up with you and Sofe in a sec, okay?" I say hastily.

I leave the locker room, come out into the schoolyard. It's lunchtime: people are sitting around on benches in the early spring sunshine, eating sandwiches, pies, pasties, doughnuts. Smells of tomato sauce and hot, flaky pastry waft toward me, and my stomach, despite the recent nausea, feels suddenly hollow. I take a deep breath and push out my abdominal muscles so that my stomach swells and hardens against the waistline of my skirt. You can do this without anyone noticing: it's a trick I discovered recently. When you suck your stomach in, it feels empty, but when you push it out, it stops rumbling (temporarily).

Anyway, I tell myself calmly, I can't eat things like pies and pasties and sandwiches anymore. Apart from the fact that they're too fattening, they've also all got wheat in them. Since last week, when I read an article in an alternative health magazine about wheat, I've cut down to eating it only once a day. The article said that it's bad for you. It bloats you up, apparently.

I lean against the brick wall of the school building in the sunshine, taking deep breaths. The trembling slows. I tell myself, *will* myself, to relax. For a moment—just a moment—I close my eyes, feeling the sun tickle my skin. The last traces of the Fear recede, and I'm safe again.

At least for a little while . . .

From the pavement, Nat's house looks achingly familiar. The white paint on the wrought-iron lace around the porch is rust-stained and peeling, and someone has used a discarded piece of wood to wedge open the window of the living room, which looks out onto the street. One of Tim's steel-cap work boots lies side down, abandoned, by the front doorstep. (The other, bewilderingly, is nowhere to be seen.)

I push open the front gate, squeeze my way past the fruit trees, shrubs, flowers, and creepers that spill riotously over the garden Nat's father works so passionately on. Not for the first time, it occurs to me how different his idea of a garden is from my parents'. Our house is all neat flower beds and fastidiously clipped, weed-free front lawn.

Today is a typical Sunday afternoon. Classical music drifts out an open window in the house across the street, and next door two men peer under the hood of a car in the driveway, beers in their hands. I walk down the mossy brick-paved driveway to the Jordans' back door. *Please don't let Nat be here. Please let her be at her boyfriend's house . . .*

Last night, I didn't sleep for hours. I sat at my desk in my bedroom, drowning in Fear: wave after wave of it. When at last it passed, everyone else had gone to bed. I stumbled down the stairs to the kitchen, opened the fridge door. I don't think I knew what I was doing: my legs felt watery beneath me, and my mind was awash with fatigue. I pulled out cheese, butter, bread, Nutella.

And I ate. Slice after slice, I ate. I couldn't seem to stop. I don't even remember what it *tasted* like.

Afterward, I put everything neatly away (what was left of it) and crept back up to my room. I lay in bed, switched off my light, stared up through the darkness to the ceiling. I counted calories over and over in my head, trying to work out how I could make up for everything I'd just consumed. My stomach felt huge, tight, swollen under my hands, but I still felt hollow inside.

Is *that* where this Fear is taking me? I can't do it anymore. I can't go there alone.

This morning, when I woke, I didn't go for a run. My stomach growled, and my body ached with tiredness and unshed tears. And I felt so *guilty.* These days, I always feel guilty about all sorts of things: whether I'm studying enough, or exercising enough; whether I'm eating too much, or sleeping too much. Sometimes I just feel guilty about whether I'm being *nice* enough to everyone. But this morning the guilt was unbearable.

That's when I thought of Nat's mother, who used to chat for hours with us whenever I came over. Who used to say to me, "If you ever need to talk about something, Lise, you only have to ask." With Nat groaning *("Mum, shut UP")* and me saying brightly, "Thanks, Mrs. Jordan. I will." Thinking, *Why does she say that to me? Does she say that to ALL Nat's friends?* I never followed her up on it, of course.

Now I push open the screen door, which is half open, and steal through the laundry room into the kitchen. Unbelievably, Nat's mother is sitting right there at the kitchen table, reading the newspaper, wrapped up in a thick quilted jacket. The house, despite the arrival of spring, still feels icy.

"Lise!" she exclaims, glancing up as I come in. Her eyes

flicker over me briefly, oddly, and then she rushes on. "How nice to see you. How *are* you?"

"Good, thank you, Mrs. Jordan," I say politely, as I always do. "How are you?"

She pushes her chair out from under the table, goes over to the kettle and switches it on, gets out the tea bags and milk. All the time she's doing this, she keeps up a stream of friendly chatter: *How are your parents? How's Terri's modeling going? Are you still enjoying running? I know how you feel; I used to LOVE it.* I'd forgotten how interested in you Nat's mum can seem to be.

"Milk?" she offers, handing me a steaming mug. "Cookie?"

I shake my head quickly. "Just black tea, thanks."

We go back over to the table together. Sitting down, Mrs. Jordan falls suddenly silent; she's waiting, I think, for me to speak. To explain why I'm here; why I haven't asked where Nat is; why I didn't just turn around and go home again when she told me Nat wasn't here. I wrap my hands around the warmth of the mug, stare down at my tea.

Now that I'm here, I don't know how to start. I'm ashamed of everything I can think of to say about myself, ashamed of all the fear. Ashamed of all this sudden *neediness.*

"What is it, my dear?" Nat's mother says finally, putting her mug back down on the table.

And it's almost as if she *knows* why I'm here.

"It's the exams," I blurt out, because this is easier to say; and because this, too, is true. "My grades have gone down this year. I think I'm going to fail."

"Are you studying enough, do you think?"

I hesitate. "Yes. No. I *think* so . . ."

I tell her my current studying timetable: an hour before school and four hours afterward, as well as all day during the weekend, including after dinner. I look at her anxiously: the thought occurs to me suddenly that maybe I *should* be squeezing more in, somehow. Then I remember that day at Nat's house—the day I went over to study with her—when Mrs. Jordan lectured me on doing too much schoolwork. She went on and on about it, to the point where I just wished she'd stop. *I KNOW I study more than most people,* I kept thinking; *I HAVE to, to keep the Fear at bay.*

But I was studying *heaps* less back then.

Now she tilts her head to one side, questioning. "What about other stuff? Is there anything else you can think of that might be affecting your marks?"

I take a breath. Now, I think. *Now* is the time to tell her. *There is this Fear,* I will say. *It gets so bad sometimes, I think there must be something wrong with me . . .*

But the words are hard to get out. They stick in my throat. I struggle desperately to speak.

"Because, you see, *I* can think of something," she continues. And she gives me that odd, flickering glance again.

I close my mouth quickly. Is it *that* obvious what's going on inside my head?

Nat's mother settles comfortably back into her chair, as if she's getting ready for a long session. She even folds her hands on her lap.

"You're very *thin* these days, Lise," she observes conversationally.

I stare at her, taken aback.

"You never used to be so thin," she goes on. "Are you sure you're eating enough?"

"Of course," I say immediately.

"It doesn't *look* like you are," she says calmly.

I rub the sole of my shoe up and down the leg of my chair, confused. This isn't at all the conversation I was planning to have with her. It's pretty ironic, really: here she is going on about my weight when that's the only thing about myself that I am sure of, the only thing I know is (sort of) okay. Can you imagine how good it feels, knowing your clothes are getting looser on you? Dropping a couple of dress sizes, feeling the way things hang so straight on you all of a sudden? It's the *best* feeling in the world. It's a feeling of—yes, *power.*

"Tell me, Lise," Mrs. Jordan says gravely, "are you on a diet?"

I shake my head quickly. "Diet": it's such a strange word, isn't it? That's what I thought this eating plan of mine was once, way back when I started it. And yet somehow, somewhere along the line, it stopped being that. Now it's just something I have to do. A set of rules I *have* to follow . . .

"Lise." Mrs. Jordan's voice breaks into my thoughts. "How much do you weigh now, exactly?"

Bingo. The million-dollar question. This morning, when I weighed myself, I was 93 pounds—down from 121 pounds at the beginning of this year. *(Yes, Mrs. Jordan, I HAVE lost weight.)* And do you know what I found out the other day? Terri's 108 pounds—15 pounds heavier than me. Isn't that bizarre? I've always thought of Terri as so *thin*.

But "thin," I've discovered, is another one of those strange words: a relative concept, not an absolute one. Recently, I've realized that what other people see as thin just isn't thin enough for me. Nowhere near. It's to do with the way you feel, I guess, rather than the way you look. And I don't feel thin yet at all.

It's not that I don't care what other people think, it's that I just can't seem to see myself as they do. And for once in my life, I want to meet my *own* expectations. I'm aiming for 90 pounds, which, by my reckoning, will look thin *on me.* Not anorexic (Jessica Fuller got way lower than that), but definitely thin.

Nat's mother sits forward in her chair.

"I asked you a question, Lise," she says sharply. The sudden sharpness bewilders me: she's always seemed so friendly before. So *nice.*

I look up at her at last, defiantly. "I don't know how much I weigh. I don't have a set of scales."

"I think you know *exactly* how much you weigh," she remarks, undeterred. "And I think you are a very hungry girl."

Her words bring a sudden stinging hotness to the back of my eyes. A voice murmurs unbidden in my mind: *I AM hungry. Can you IMAGINE how hungry I am?* I swallow, hard. This is *not* what I came here to talk to her about. I thought she was on my side.

"Lise . . ."

I wait, wary now.

"You have to *do* something about this."

I don't say anything.

"Have you discussed this with your parents at all? Your mother?"

I shake my head, horrified at the thought.

She sighs. "Lise, I think you need help." She spreads her hands out on the table before me, palms down, firm. "I'm really worried about you. You need to see a counselor, or a doctor. I can give you some names, if you like."

I shrug. She can give me all the names she likes. What help are they? I thought she said that *she* would talk to me.

"Lise," Mrs. Jordan says again. "There's something I have to tell you." She leans back in her chair, arms folded across her chest. "If you won't do anything yourself, I'm going to have to speak to your parents. Not today. Not tomorrow. But soon. You're not well, my dear. I have no choice." She nods firmly. "You need help."

Something creaks then, in the laundry room or up on the roof. I struggle to speak, to say *Please don't,* or *You can't,* or *At least not my MOTHER. PLEASE not my mother.* Again, no words come out.

And it's then that we both become aware of someone standing in the doorway to the kitchen.

"Lise!" Nat exclaims, coming in. "What're you doing here?"

I push back my chair hastily. My cheeks are burning. How long was she standing there in the laundry room? How much of our conversation did she hear?

"I came over . . . I forgot that you'd be at Josh's . . . I've just had a cup of tea . . . ," I stammer.

"I should've been back ages ago," she admits ruefully. She glances curiously back and forth, from her mother to me. Then she says awkwardly to me, "How *are* you, anyway?"

"All right," I say stiffly.

I can feel that I'm still blushing. The conversation between us feels heavy and stilted, as if we haven't spoken to each other for months. Actually, we probably haven't—not properly, anyway. Not as best *friends.*

"How's Josh?" Nat's mother asks her quickly.

Nat turns to answer her.

"Okay." She pulls a face. "I had to tell him I can't see him for a while. He's stopping me from getting any studying done. I can't concentrate when I know I'm going to see him."

Mrs. Jordan smiles knowingly.

Nat colors. "It's just—the exams're getting so *close.*"

And this is the cue I have been looking for. Thank God, thank *God,* a cue. I scramble up from my chair.

Nat looks surprised. "You off already? Don't you want to stay?"

"I can't," I say, with what I hope is a convincingly apologetic look on my face. "I've got that math assignment still to do . . ."

"Not even for a second cup of tea?" says Mrs. Jordan.

They are both facing me now, waiting.

"I *can't,*" I repeat frantically. "I've got so much to do . . ."

Neither of them moves to follow me out. In my haste, I let the screen door bang loudly behind me as I leave, but I ignore it and don't look back. As I hurry up the driveway, a stray branch from a creeper brushes against my face. The feel of it on my skin startles me: its leaves are rain-wet, heavy, fat with luxuriant growth. I think longingly of my mother's barren lawn.

Back in the safety of my own bedroom, I sit at my desk, staring at the studying schedule pinned up on the corkboard above it.

I lied to Mrs. Jordan. In her way, my mother *has* spoken to me. When I lost those first few pounds, she praised me: *See what a little cutting back can do?* Now, though, at dinner, she says things like *Have a little more, Lise. You make me feel guilty.* As if *her* struggle with chocolate bars is *my* fault. *That's* what my mother says to me.

Sometimes, as we eat, I look in the mirror on the wall opposite the stainless steel countertop, see her eyes flicking between Terri and me, measuring, weighing up, *comparing.* This is nothing new: she's done it all my life. If she's worried, as Mrs. Jordan seems to think she should be, it doesn't show. *I weigh less than Terri now,* I whisper silently each night to my mother's reflection in the mirror. *I know it doesn't LOOK like it, but I DO.*

But her eyes are down on her scraped-clean plate. Her fingers drum their cigarette cravings out on the stainless steel, and she doesn't look up.

And this is proof to me that I haven't gotten there yet: that despite all this weight I've lost, I'm still. Not. *Thin.*

Will Nat's mother ring my parents? After all these years,

after all those promises, I can't believe that's all she had to offer me. It doesn't make sense. Hunger is the least of my problems.

And if *she* can't help, who can? Let's face it, the next time the Fear hits, I'm all on my own.

Again . . .

chapter twenty-two

Suspended

One Monday morning, three weeks before the pre-exam study week, Sofia turns up at Assembly with her nose pierced.

The school, of course, goes into immediate uproar. You're not allowed to get your nose pierced; you're not allowed to get *anything* pierced, really, except your ears. And even with earrings, you're only supposed to wear one on each side.

"They'll make you take it out, you know," Nat warns her as we file out of Assembly.

Sofia rolls her eyes. "There's only three weeks until we leave this place. And anyway, I can't *possibly* take it out, because the hole will close up."

"Does Nick like it?"

Sofia pushes her ponytail impatiently behind her shoulder. "Don't know. Haven't asked."

"What about your mum?" I ask curiously.

Sofia shrugs. "Mum's cool. She doesn't hassle me about stuff like that."

But if her mother doesn't hassle her, Miss George, the headmistress, does. Halfway through the first lesson, Sofia receives a message to report immediately to the front office. And at recess, when I next see her, she's kneeling at her locker, packing her schoolbag, a truculent expression on her face.

"I'm suspended," she says tersely, before I can ask. "Until I take it out."

At these words, a crowd gathers quickly around her in the locker room.

"Suspended?"

"For a *nose ring*?"

"That is just *so* typical."

Ignoring everyone else, Sofia stands up. She slings her bag over her shoulder, starts walking toward the door. As she reaches the entrance, someone calls out brightly, "Why didn't you get your belly button done instead?"

Sofia swings around, glaring. "What for? I like *nose* rings."

"Yeah, but no one'd be able to *see* a belly-button ring."

Sofia groans and turns away again. "What kind of Nazi place *is* this, anyway? It's *my* body and *my* choice."

And she walks out of the locker room.

Nat and I exchange glances. We run hastily after her, out into the schoolyard.

"*Sofe.* You're not *really* going to let yourself get suspended now."

"There's only four weeks left till the exams . . ."

"Oh, piss *off,* the pair of you," Sofia says irritably. She stops walking. "Listen, I'll be back in a couple of days, all right? *Minus* the nose ring. I'm not that stupid. I just thought . . ." And here a slow, cheeky grin starts to spread across her face. "I just thought I might as well make the most of it. I don't think I've ever actually been offered a couple of days off school before."

She starts to walk off again, then stops, swings back around, comes over to me. Standing in front of me, feet firmly planted on the ground, she reaches out, prods me in the stomach. She looks at me, hard.

"Oy. You. *Eat.*"

Then she strolls casually out of the yard, nose ring glinting triumphantly in the sun.

chapter twenty-three

Afternoon tea at the Mawsons'

That same week, summer hits. The sun glares on the pages of our textbooks during lessons, and flies buzz thickly at the classroom windows. Sometimes they drop onto our desks out of midair, landing heavily, legs up, having died in midflight.

I stare out the windows, shading my forehead with my hand from the light, unable to concentrate. Has Mrs. Jordan rung yet? What will she say? What will my parents say? Light trickles through the gaps between my fingers, hostile and hot on my skin. I turn back to my notebook, eyes dazzled, burning.

Starting from that week, I begin walking home instead of catching the bus. Partly, I've decided to do this to get more exercise; partly, to avoid the company of Nat. Ever since that day we went shopping together—ever since the strange, silent bus trip home—she's been difficult to be with, asking constant, awkward questions like "Is everything all right,

Lise? You look so *pale.*" Or else looking at me strangely and saying nothing at all.

Sometimes, these days, I'd almost rather be with Sofia than Nat. I used to be so afraid of Sofe: of not being able to think of anything to say to her; of feeling hopeless, *inadequate,* in front of her. But since I've lost weight, that's changed. It's not that I've got more to say to her, because I haven't: I still feel tongue-tied in her company. It's just, I don't know—I don't *care* so much. Despite what she said to me that dreadful morning at Nat's house on my birthday, I've done something she can't: I've gotten fit, gotten (well, *almost*) slim. I've gotten *disciplined.* And that's something she can't take away from me. No matter how many times she tells me to eat.

There's usually no one home when I turn in at the front gate and crunch my way down the gravel drive. Mum and Dad don't tend to leave work until well after five, and it would tarnish Terri's "cool uni student" image if she got home before dark. So the house is empty, and I rattle around in the kitchen, enjoying the sound of my feet echoing on the wooden floorboards. My latest ritual is to open all the cupboard doors and check the fridge, gaze longingly at the containers of leftovers and Terri's jar of Nutella.

There has been no repeat of that midnight binge. Now, on out-of-control days, I pull out the block of cheese, put it on the countertop, cut myself the tiniest shaving. The sharp, rich taste makes me dream of toasted sandwiches, cheeseburgers, my mother's homemade lasagna . . .

Then I make myself a cup of green tea (good for the digestion, apparently—and, of course, it has no calories) and wander up the stairs to my room to study. All the time I'm settling down at my desk, opening my books, checking my studying schedule, there's this little panicked whisper inside my head: *I've got to study more. I'm going to fail.*

But one afternoon, when I get home from school, Mum's sleek silver car and Dad's BMW are parked at the end of the driveway. My heart sinks, and I walk through the kitchen door slowly, practicing *Smile, Lise, smile.*

"How about some afternoon tea?" Mum suggests brightly, pecking me on the cheek. "I've just made a banana cake."

Imagine: Mum *baking.* What's gotten into her? I wonder. She stopped doing that when I was in kindergarten. I inspect her closely: there's a spot of bare skin on her chin where she must have missed her foundation, and the mascara on her eyelashes is clumpy. Mum *never* botches her makeup.

Has Mrs. Jordan finally rung? Is that what she's so upset about?

Dad's perched on a barstool at the countertop, buried in a medical journal. He smiles up at me as I put my schoolbag down.

"Jen made the cake specially, Lisey."

Specially for *what*? To make me fat? I shake my head at the cake (imagine: *me* eating cake. I stopped doing that *months* ago) and head instead to the kettle. While I wait for it to boil, I fidget around in the cupboards, getting out a cup, cutting a slice of lemon. All the time I'm doing this, I try not to breathe in too deeply: the kettle sits next to the oven, from which the most incredible, sweet warm-cake smells are drifting out.

Hastily, I pick my cup up, ready to take it back to my room with me to study.

"Lise . . . ," says Mum.

I stop. *Here it comes . . .*

"You know how you told me you've been having trouble sleeping?"

I nod, cautiously. I mentioned it to her the other day, when she told me off at the dinner table for yawning all the time.

"Well . . . I got something. To help." She looks at me worriedly. "I know you're into herbal things, so I bought it from the health food shop."

"*Health* food shop," my father mutters scornfully, going back to his journal.

She ignores him pointedly and hands me a brown paper bag. I put down my cup again, relieved: if that's all she's going to say, I can handle it. Maybe Nat's mother kept quiet after all. Calmly, I open the bag. Inside, there's a packet of valerian tea bags and a CD—one of those do-it-yourself meditation/relaxation CDs.

Oh, Mum. I stare down at the brown paper bag, breath suddenly catching, unable to speak. The gesture is so unlike my mother (who couldn't relax if you paid her to), and so close to the bone, that I'm overwhelmed. For one long, insane moment, all I want to do is curl up on my mother's lap and bawl my eyes out. *If she only knew . . .*

Because the truth is, every night now I struggle to sleep. It's become the time of day I most dread: a time when the Fear hits and there is no one to talk to, nothing to distract myself with. I try everything: listening to the radio, playing solitaire, reading recipes. Nothing works. Sometimes I have to get up and pace my room, fighting my way through bout after bout of it.

And when the Fear has finally run its course and I do eventually get to sleep, I dream about food: Nat's chocolate cake, iced with dark, thick, glossy icing, smothered with cream; bread spread with butter an inch thick; hot chips, salty and sharp and fragrant with vinegar. I wake up in the morning, stomach growling, the memory of food guilty on my tongue.

Mum, Mum, I can't sleep, and I can't eat, and I can't talk to boys, and I can't talk to my best friend anymore, and I feel so goddamn LONELY . . .

I look up at her, heart brimming. But then, just as I'm about to speak, I notice the way her stomach, tightly corseted by her short, narrow skirt, bulges underneath the waistband. Instantly I am diverted. *How can she LIVE with herself?* I wonder. *How can she handle the way her stomach sticks out like that? Why can't she show some self-control?*

Dad's no better, either. His belly sags over his trousers, and his chin is receding into his neck. In the mornings, when he scoots back from the bathroom to the bedroom after a shower, towel wrapped around his waist, you can see the way the skin on his back hangs slack and his hips, above the folded-over top of the towel, are loose with middle-aged midriff flab.

And they're not the only ones. Lately I've been seeing fat people everywhere I look: people with cellulite-hatched thighs, droopy breasts, swollen stomachs. It doesn't seem to matter whether I'm looking at strangers or at friends. The other day I even checked out Sofia—yes, Sofia, the *ultimate* boy magnet—and realized what a big butt she has. The whole world seems suddenly to be full of people who have too much flesh, people who spend the day stuffing themselves with food. Why didn't I ever notice this before?

Dad's still reading, but Mum's eyes are fixed anxiously on me, as if she's waiting—*hoping,* even—for me to spill the magic beans, confess my dreaded secret so she can make it all better. But the moment of weakness has passed, and I'm strong again. I am *not* going to confide in my overweight, dimply-thighed, sweaty-cleavaged mother.

"Thanks for the CD, Mum," I say quickly, heading toward the kitchen door, toward sweet, beckoning escape. "It's really nice of you."

For a moment, I think I might get there. But I don't even make it past the oven.

"Your father and I need to talk to you, Lise," says Mum abruptly.

I lean against the oven door, cup in hand, suddenly trapped.

"What about?" I say quietly, knowing already. So Mrs. Jordan *did* ring. I should have known she wouldn't let me go.

Mum turns to Dad expectantly. He gazes back at her, not saying anything, a page of his medical journal between his fingers.

"Rob."

"What?"

"*You're* the doctor."

He doesn't answer.

"You *promised*—"

Dad sighs, exasperated. He lets the page of his journal drop.

"I didn't promise anything. I said I'd *be* here—"

Mum goes red in the face with anger. She swings back to me.

"I had a call from Natalie's mother last night." Her voice is harsh, offended: she and Nat's mother have never gotten on. "She said—"

"This has nothing to do with Nell Jordan," Dad says.

They glare at each other. Antagonism—heavy, unbidden—hangs suddenly in the air. I watch them, feeling the warmth of the oven door against my back, pushing myself farther into it. I *hate* the way they argue like this.

Mum faces me again, the anger still red in her face.

"It's time you stopped losing weight, Lise," she says brusquely. "You've lost enough already."

I don't speak. I am starting to sweat, a warm, moist patch forming under the back of my sweater, where I'm leaning against the oven. Is this all anyone's *ever* going to talk to me about?

"You're too thin," Mum goes on. Her voice rises, on the lower rung of hysteria. "*Look* at you! You look unhealthy."

"I'm not!" I protest hotly. "I *don't.*" I turn to my father, appealing to his better—his more reasonable—nature. "Dad?"

"Rob," says Mum. This time it is a command.

His eyes on me are apologetic. "You *do* look a bit thin, Lisey. Enough is enough."

I go over to the sink, put my cup of cold green tea down on the draining board. My hands are shaking. Part of me is exultant—*Yes,* I'm *thin*! They *said* I'm thin!—but the other part feels suddenly afraid. What if they make me gain weight? What if they make me get *fat*?

"I'm okay. Honestly. It's just the exams."

"Terri never got like this about the exams," Mum snaps.

Oh, yes: the old Terri trick. But Terri's *smart*! I think. Terri's brainy. And Terri's never *needed* to lose weight. I mean, look at her: she's even got part-time modeling work now.

Mum folds her arms, determined now. "I'm going to book an appointment with a doctor—"

"But Dad's a doctor!" I protest. "*He* didn't say I look unhealthy."

And he didn't: he just said I looked a little *thin*. There's nothing wrong with *thin*.

Dad looks puzzled, out of his depth. "I wouldn't go as far as 'unhealthy' Lisey. Not *medically* speaking—"

"You see?" I say triumphantly to my mother.

Just then, the alarm on the oven goes off. It beeps insistently into the silence between us. Mum rushes over to it. She switches it off and opens the oven door. Instantly we are bathed in the warm, loving smell of freshly baked cake. Despite myself, I breathe in deeply, savoring the smell, tasting its sweetness at the back of my throat.

Mum and Dad, too, have stopped. Their faces soften; Dad is on the verge of a smile.

"That smells great, Jen."

"Does it?" Her shoulders drop, the tension gone, and she gives him a silly, pleased look. "It's my normal recipe—you know, the one with the cardamom in it. I was going to put some cream-cheese icing on it when it's cooled."

"Can't we have it now?" Suddenly he sounds almost boyish, mischievous. "Come on, Jen. Let's have some *now.*"

"Well . . ." She hesitates.

Dad turns to me. "Lise? You'll have some, won't you? If we cut it now?"

I glance at the cake. It smells so good. But I can't; I *can't*—

And that's when I think of it. The answer to everything, the perfect solution . . .

Upstairs, I sit at my bedroom desk. The cake I've just eaten lies heavy in my stomach. *It doesn't matter,* I tell myself over and over, trying to rid myself of the old, familiar guilt. *It was only this once. And it was worth it to get my parents off my back. I'll just have to run extra hard tomorrow morning to make up for it.*

"If I have some now," I said to them back there in the kitchen, "will you forget about the appointment you were going to make with the doctor?"

I can still see their faces when I suggested it: searching,

trying to figure me out, not coming up with anything concrete. Finally, they had to agree. They had no reason to disbelieve me. And besides, I even made a promise.

"I'll have a piece every afternoon. When I come home from school. If you leave some cake out for me, I'll have it, I swear."

What could they say? They pulled their stools up to the countertop, gestured to me to join them. I can still see it now: Mum cutting the cake—slowly, reverently; Dad looking at Mum in the mirror, stupid with *I-told-you-so* relief. Both of them watching me eat.

The cake was sticky. I could taste the bananas in it, overripe and cloyingly sweet. A lump of it sat in the back of my throat, making it hard to swallow. And there was something else clotting my throat, too: something akin to anger, to tears. I could have eaten the whole *thing*. In one sitting, I could have eaten that cake.

"Thanks, Mum. That was delicious. Thank you *both* for coming home for afternoon tea today."

They won't be home tomorrow afternoon, of course. Not tomorrow, or the next day, or the day after that. Today was a one-off—a day sneaked from the office in the name of their daughter's health. Tomorrow they will be back at work, making up for lost time—lost sales, abandoned patients—and I will be alone in the house. Me and my slice of banana cake, crumbling, crumbling, into the rubbish bin.

I take out the box of tea bags Mum gave me, read the instructions on it thoroughly. Then I put it on my bedside table. According to the nutritional analysis on the back of the box, they have no calories, so perhaps they're worth a try. I'd give *anything* for a good night's sleep.

But I put the meditation CD in the bottom drawer of my desk. I don't *want* to "sit still and let my thoughts go," as the blurb on the cover suggests. I can't think of anything *worse.* When I let my thoughts go, they drift and wheel and return to me, full of hunger, and longing, and guilt.

And huge, black Fear.

chapter twenty-four

Jessica

The last day of Year 12 is a tradition at our school. Not only is there just the one week of studying left before the exams, but it's also the last day of secondary education forever. And who knows what will come next?

Our year is no different from any of the others before it. All day, my classmates run around the schoolyard squirting each other (and everyone else) with shaving cream. They tear up each other's uniforms and autograph them, and then race up the stairs to the top of the science building, throwing flour bombs at teachers and students passing below. They sing rude songs at the top of their voices and write swear-words on the covers of their prayer books.

And some people have their own private rebellions, too. Sofia, for example, disappears at lunchtime and returns an hour later with her nose repierced.

"Got it done at the hairdresser's down the road this time," she tells everyone, grinning. "They can't expel me now."

"Did it hurt?" someone asks.

She shrugs. "It was worth it. Mate, I am *so* not going to miss this place."

It's about then that I creep away from everyone else and retreat into the school library. I've tried to get into the spirit of things, *tried* to join in. But my heart isn't in it: I don't feel remotely like celebrating. Apart from the fact that I can't get the exams off my mind (*I'm-going-to-fail-I'm-going-to-fail-I'm-going-to-FAIL*), I, unlike the others, *will* miss school.

Because despite the loneliness I often feel here—the feeling of not being like anyone else; the feeling of not being *liked* by anyone else (even my best friend)—at least here I am accepted. People put up with me; I know what I'm supposed to do each day; I know where I fit in.

And I'm not sure that's going to happen once I've left this school. Not sure at all . . .

It's not until just after lunch, when we're all back at the locker room changing out of our uniforms and cleaning our lockers out before leaving, that Nat, Sofe, and I finally converge on each other.

"You want to go out for a coffee?" Nat suggests, shoving pens, paper, and loose-leaf notebooks into her bag. "To celebrate?"

Sofia glances through the window at the blue sky. "Let's go and sit on the grass in the park, hey. It's too nice to sit in a coffee shop."

We walk out of the schoolyard together. Sofia and Nat

take their backpacks with them, staggering slightly under their weight. I leave mine in my locker, planning to come back via the school on the way home: there are still some textbooks I need to borrow from the library for studying. We stroll down the road, soaking up the sun. It's the first time in weeks that the three of us have been together.

"I can't believe it's the exams in one week's time," says Nat as we reach the entrance to the park. "I'm nowhere near ready for them, you know? I even had to ask Michael to give me time off work until they're over. And I made Josh promise not to see me till then, either."

Sofia rolls her eyes. "They're only exams."

"Yeah, but I've left everything to the last moment. I mean like—everything." Nat sighs. "I'll never get into uni now. I'm just hoping I'll *pass*."

We wander over to a gum tree on the far side of the park and settle down underneath it, not far from a set of rusted, empty swings and a seesaw with paint flaking off it. When I was younger, mothers used to bring their kids to this park to play on the swings, and families set up their grills and had barbecues by the creek. Nat and I used to come here, too, for picnics on warm spring weekends. We'd drink lemonade and watch the magpies ferret in the earth with their beaks for worms. And we'd talk and talk and talk.

But things change. In the last few years, the park has fallen out of community favor for some reason. (Fashion, maybe; or different people moving into the area; or the new shopping complex just down the road, which has a McDonald's playground out front.) There are even rumors that the toilets are used as a pickup spot for gay men and that drug dealers come here to deal. And today, just like any other day—despite the beautiful weather, despite the neatly mown grass and the brightly colored flowers planted by the city along the perimeter—there's no one else in sight.

"I can't wait till next year," says Sofia, rolling lazily onto her back.

Nat's lying on her stomach, her legs kicking the air. "Have you made up your mind where you want to do your nursing?"

"I've decided not to go straight into study next year after all," says Sofia. "I'm deferring for a year. Nick and I're going to buy an old VW van and travel around Australia. Do some volunteer work on organic farms. Stuff like that."

"Really?" Nat nudges her elbow into Sofia's ribs, grinning. "You little hippie, you."

The only one still sitting up, I cross my legs, feet tucked under my knees, studying a caterpillar that's inching its way across the dry, crackly gum leaves at my feet. I read somewhere recently that caterpillars eat several times their body weight every day until they go into their chrysalis. Imagine, I think longingly, if humans could eat that much and not get fat. Imagine how blissfully *full* you'd feel . . .

Nat sighs again. "I haven't even thought about next year. I just want the exams to be over, you know? So I can catch up with Josh. Get on with my life."

"What about you, Lise?" says Sofia drowsily. "You still planning to do law?"

"Of course she's still planning to do law," Nat says before I can answer. "She's been wanting to do it for the last five *years.*"

I pick up a twig, trace a pattern with it in the dusty soil. "I might not get in, you know."

Sofia and Nat make puking noises. "Yeah, right, Lise. As *if.*"

Sun-spotted shadows from the gum leaves above us dance across my skin. *Law.* It seems so far away, so unreal. And so unlikely. *Is* that what I'll be doing next year? Is it what I *want* to do next year? I wish I could explain to them how the thought of it—the thought of *anything* beyond this safe, warm (Fear-driven) little world I live in now—fills me with dread . . .

I close my eyes, the air warm against my cheek. Today should be a good day, I remind myself sternly, trying to lift myself out of the blackness: today I hit 90 pounds. My target. And yet the strange thing is, I don't feel any different from how I felt yesterday, or last week, or last month. I still feel fat. I still *look* fat.

I stare up at the swaying trunk of the gum tree. *Maybe I should try for 85 pounds?* I think idly. And a little flutter of excitement goes through me, the first of the day. Think about it: going *under* 90 pounds. Now *that's* thin.

Sofia yawns. "I could just go to sleep . . . ," she says, closing her eyes.

Nat, too, is yawning. She rests her head on her arms, legs finally still. "Me, too."

Their faces are shadow-brushed and peaceful. After a moment, I lie down on my back next to them. Closing my eyes, I fold my arms across my middle: protecting my stomach, keeping it warm. Shielding its discontented rumblings from the companionable silence that has slipped slowly, pleasurably, among us. And for a moment, lying there, I could almost believe that nothing has changed. That you can still hear the sound of barbecues sizzling, of children shrieking on the swings. That hunger means nothing more than that tiny gap between a midafternoon ice cream and the evening meal. And that Nat and I still talk . . .

A piece of bark dislodges itself suddenly from the top of the tree trunk, making a small, sharp, crackling sound that jolts me awake. I open my eyes, watch it rustle through the leaves and drop to the ground next to me. Wide awake again, I roll over onto my stomach. I stare intently at the ground, willing myself not to look up again through the leaves to the top of the tree and beyond, where the sky yawns at me, a distant, empty blue.

"Lise?"

I'm standing in the school library, leaning against a bookshelf, deeply ensconced in the Year 12 biology textbook's version of human anatomy, when I hear my name. Still somewhere amidst atria and ventricles, I lift my head, startled. I thought everyone else had gone home; I said goodbye to Nat and Sofia at the school gate ages ago. But I was wrong, I realize slowly: it's Jessica Fuller, and she's coming over to me.

"Lise?" She says my name again quietly, almost hesitantly, even though—apart from the school librarian—there's no one else here. "I've been looking for you everywhere. I just wanted to say . . . good luck. With the exams."

I close the book in my hands and turn to face her, surprised. This must be the first thing she's ever said to me one-on-one. Jessica belongs to the "trendy" set—the group of girls who hang out in Rundle Mall on Friday nights and go out with gorgeous, popular boys from other private schools. People like Jessica just don't *talk* to people like me.

I examine her more closely. She's so pretty, with her thick blond hair, the tiny waist, her long, slim legs. And she's so popular. *Everyone* likes Jessica Fuller.

"Good luck to you, too," I say awkwardly, not knowing what else to say. Surely she hasn't been looking for me all over the school to say *that*?

There's a pause. She bites her lip. "What I really wanted to say . . ."

But her voice trails off, her cheeks flooding with color.

"The thing is," she blurts out finally, "you just can't take exams on an empty stomach, Lise. You've got to *eat*."

I stare at her. My mind starts chattering noisily. Who's *she* to talk? She's lost heaps of weight again since she came out of the hospital at the end of last year. Oh, she doesn't look as if she's at death's door anymore, but she's much thinner than she was *before* she became anorexic. And she still doesn't eat very much, you know. I've seen her at lunchtime, scrumpling up bits of sandwiches in plastic wrap, stuffing them into the bin.

"I'm sorry," Jessica says. "I know you think it's none of my business. It's just . . ." She hesitates again, and then says, with sudden, alarming passion, "I can't *stand* seeing someone else make the same mistake as I did. I can't stand watching you *do* this to yourself."

My breath catches. "I'm fine," I say quickly. "You don't need to worry. I eat fine."

She looks me over without speaking, and it feels as if her eyes are scanning my body, detecting parts of me that even I'm not aware of.

"It doesn't matter *how* thin you get, you know," she says then, quietly. "Trust me. The way you feel about yourself—it doesn't change. It just *doesn't*. You *still* don't feel like an okay person. You never do."

Her words clutch at me. It feels as if she's inside my head. *She knows,* I think incredulously, staring down at the carpet. *She knows what this FEELS like. She knows what I'm THINKING.*

The thought terrifies me. And suddenly—I don't know—I feel like crying. Yet again. What has gotten into me recently?

"Listen . . ." Jessica reaches out, rests her hand lightly for a second on my wrist. "If you ever want to talk to someone, I'm here, okay?"

Her touch almost undoes me. I stare downward into nothingness, trying not to blink, forcing myself to wait the moment out, to see my way through my swimming eyes.

No one *ever* touches me; not even my parents. I just . . . I'm not a huggy person. I don't *do* touchy-feely.

She reaches into her pocket, hands me a piece of paper with her name and phone number on it. Then she turns away, starts to leave. Halfway to the library door, she turns back.

"It takes one to know one, Lise," she says simply.

chapter twenty-five

Exams

On the day of the first exam, I wake up with a feeling of utter, soulless dread. I get up, put on my running gear, creep out of the house. When I start to run, my feet hit the cracked asphalt pavement, dull and heavy. (Yes, at a little under 90 pounds I'm *still* too heavy.) I run in slow, tired rhythm: *I'm-going-to-fail-I'm-going-to-fail-I'm-going-to-fail* . . .

Afterward, in the shower, I inspect myself. It's bizarre. I can *see* I've lost weight: my hip bones jut out, and my thighs don't rub together anymore, and I can circle my finger and thumb halfway up my forearm. You can see the shadow of my ribs, too, through my skin—not sharp, not pointed, but there. *Mine.* I am no longer made up of curves: just nice, straight lines.

But it's still not enough. I still don't feel okay.

On the way out of the kitchen, I pass Terri eating breakfast at the counter. She yawns up at me, her mouth full of toasted muesli.

"First one today?"

I nod. "English."

I hover at the other end of the counter, fiddling with Mum's cigarette packet by the phone. The cereal box stands next to Terri's elbow, and for one long, longing moment I dream: of crunchy oats and dried fruit; of the leftover milk at the bottom of the bowl that you spoon up, all sweet and sugary and warm.

And then I just . . . let the thought go. I decided last night that the only way to get through these exams now is to fast before each one. Fasting clears your mind, I read somewhere: it calms you down, sharpens your thought processes. I could do with a bit of that.

"Good luck, Lisa-lou," Terri says sleepily.

I nod, take a deep breath, and step outside.

The unopened exam paper on my desk is pink. I notice this as I stare down at it. No one told me it would be pink, I think incongruously; the practice papers were white.

Sunlight pours through the classroom window: it cascades into a bright patch on the floor, motes of dust dancing in its path. My heart is racing and my hands are clammy. *I'll be all right,* I tell myself, over and over. *I'll be all right.*

I glance across at Nat, who's sitting beside me, and then at Sofia, in front. On my other side is Anna Chan. The familiar sight of her sleek black hair, gathered in its customary ponytail, comforts me momentarily. *I'll be all right.*

"You may begin, girls," says Mrs. Lovett.

I open the writing booklet, pick up my pen. I stare at the pages of the exam paper—a sea of blurred pale pink—and a wave of sickness hits me from nowhere. *Oh, God. Oh, God. Please don't let this happen now . . .*

My heart zigzags, skips a beat, lurches crazily in my throat. I clutch my desk. Sweat beads spring up at my temples. I take a deep breath, come up for air again, swallow wildly. *This will go away.*

But it doesn't. A hot, choking tide of nausea engulfs me, and . . . *I'm NOT all right. I never was and I never will be . . .* My pen clatters to the floor. I am drowning in sickness and fear.

And then I am up, pushing my chair back, stumbling past desk upon pink-paged desk. Past rows of upturned, curious faces and Mrs. Lovett's startled, worried gesturing. I shake my head: *No, no, leave me alone . . .* Opening the door. Out of the room. Running, now. Running.

And all the way, these huge, stupid, uncontrollable sobs tearing at my throat, like wild, clawing beasts finally let loose.

PART V

Nat

chapter twenty-six

Not all right

Out of the corner of my eye, I see her. She jumps up in the middle of the exam room, her chair spilling back, and she's making this funny, gasping, choking sound. The moment that it takes for her to push her way past all the desks to the front of the room seems to last forever.

Then she's like—*gone.* She doesn't come back.

After the exam's over, people mill around in the schoolyard, chatting. ("What did you put for question nine?" "How many pages did you write?" "I just *know* I failed . . .") As usual, the people who think they've done brilliantly wail that they haven't, while the people who've failed stay knowingly, stoically quiet. Personally, I'm just glad it's over, and that it wasn't as hard as I thought it would be.

I hang around with everyone else for a while, talking. But all the time, in the back of my mind, the questions keep circling: *What happened to Lise? What was WRONG?*

She looked *shocking* this morning. The last time I'd seen her before today was a week ago, at the park. Then she was pale and thin, but sort of okay, you know?—in a fragile, undernourished kind of way. Today, before the exam, she looked—hell, I don't know *how* to describe the way she looked. It wasn't just that she's lost more weight over this last week (although I'm sure she has, a little). There were huge, dark shadows underneath her eyes, like she hadn't slept in days, and she had this weird, haunted expression on her face. It was like she was terrified. Of what, I don't know.

Sofia makes her way across the schoolyard to me as I'm mulling this over.

"How'd you do?"

"Okay," I say, distracted.

"I bet Josh'll be dying to hear how you did. You dropping in on him this afternoon?"

"I told you before, Sofe—I haven't seen him for *weeks,*" I say crossly. "We call each other, but that's it. Till the exams're finished."

She sighs dreamily. "I don't know how you do it. I can't go without Nick for more than a couple of *days.*"

"I didn't say I didn't miss him."

I *do* miss Josh. When I speak to him on the phone, I long for him so much it feels like he's almost *there* with me—like he's lying next to me, holding me, touching my face. His voice in my ear sounds teddy-bear soft.

"You want to go out for a coffee?" says Sofia. "You don't have an exam this afternoon, right?"

It's tempting, but I shake my head.

"Did you see Lise?" I ask instead.

She nods. "That was weird, hey. She just *ran*."

"D'you think she's all right?"

Sofia gives me an impatient scowl. "What do *you* think? She hasn't been all right all year."

She's right, of course.

"I can't stop thinking about her, you know?" I say helplessly. "If I could just talk to her—"

I keep thinking—if only I could have stopped this from happening to Lise; if only I could have made things all right for her. *Completely* all right, I mean: not just today, but the whole lot of it—the whole year. If I could just make Lise *Lise* again—

Dad's in the garden when I get home, puttering around, tying heat-bedraggled tomato plants onto bamboo stakes. He greets me with a smile as I come through the gate.

"Exam go all right, Nat?"

I nod, preoccupied. "Is Mum home yet?"

"She got back a while ago," he says. "She's in the kitchen, I think."

I go straight in. *Lise,* I've been thinking; *maybe Mum can tell me what to do about Lise.*

But when I tell her what's happened, she doesn't seem surprised.

"What a shame," she just says sadly. "I did wonder . . ."

She lapses into silence, twines her fingers around her glass of wine, holds its coolness up to her cheek. I sit there opposite her at the kitchen table, waiting for her to speak. Warm late-afternoon air drifts over us from the open window.

"Call her," Mum says finally. "That's what you should do, Nat." She nods firmly. *"Call her."*

I shift restlessly in my chair. "You think?"

Images wheel through my head: Lise brandishing the *Cruelty to Animals* videotape, saying, "Think of all the *weight* we could lose." Lise complaining about the clothes that day we went shopping: "But they make me look so *fat*!" Lise running out of the exam room, skinny arms flailing, cheeks soaked with tears. She hardly *ever* cries, Lise.

Mum's right, of course, I think. I *should* call Lise. That's what friendship's about, isn't it? Talking to each other; being there for each other—just *being* there. Like I should have been for Lise before. Before, when it still wasn't too late—

"She must be feeling very lonely right now," Mum goes on, persuasively. "She probably needs someone to talk to."

Someone to talk to.

Something shifts inside me then: a memory, half forgotten, shoved to the back of my mind; a puzzle whose pieces never quite fit. That day I came home and found Lise in the kitchen, talking to Mum. I remember how surprised I was: *What's LISE doing, talking to HER when I'm not here?* I stood in the laundry room, bewildered, unable to move, and I heard Mum saying something like *I think you need help, Lise.*

But that was *weeks* ago. If Mum knew Lise needed help back then, why didn't she do something?

I can feel a bubbling starting inside of me. For years

now, I have always assumed my mother knew best. She's the social worker, remember? Oh, I've laughed at her, made fun of her psychological "insights," resented her efforts to be "deep" with my friends. I've yelled at her for being nosy, digging things out of people; for insisting that you should "confront truth" and "resolve conflict." Those neat, professional phrases she uses: I've gone around deliberately doing the opposite of what she'd advise, just because she bugs me so much.

But in my heart, I've always thought she was right. That's why she bugs me so much, you know?—because she's always so inescapably *right.*

I stare at her now across the table (our famous "round" table). Anger goes on rising in me, swift and astonishing. She *knew* about Lise. She knew all along—

"Why don't *you* call Lise?" I say slowly.

Mum stares at me, bewildered. *"Me?"*

For one moment—for one long moment—I hesitate. I'm a conflict *avoider,* right? Then I take a deep, angry breath. *Not anymore, I'm not.*

"Yeah, you, Mum," I say savagely. "*You're* the one she comes and talks to, aren't you? You're her special friend. *You* talk to her."

Mum sucks in her breath, short and sharp.

"Lise isn't my 'special friend,' Nat," she says. "I'm sorry if you feel that way, but—"

I interrupt her, my voice rising.

"I heard you talking to her that day she came over. What did she say to you?"

She shakes her head. "I can't tell you that. It was private. What she told me, she told me in confidence."

"Private." "In confidence." There they are again, more of her beautiful catchall phrases. I am so sick of her soothing terminology, her simple little solutions.

I push my chair away from the table, stand up. Anger washes over me now in strange, hot waves.

"How can you say that?" I shout. "*Look* at her. She's wasting away! What's private about *that*?"

We stare at each other across the room.

"Nat," says Mum. She gestures to me, a small, familiar conciliatory gesture: *Come back. Let's talk about this.* But there is no way I am talking to her about this. There is no way I'm talking to her about *anything.*

I move hastily away from her. In the doorway, I turn back.

"You should've done something, Mum," I say bitterly. "She came to you, and she trusted you. You should've *done* something."

Then I turn and walk out of the room.

My mother, the social worker. The so-called expert. How could she have gotten things so *wrong*?

chapter twenty-seven

Josh

That night, I dream of Josh. I dream he's riding into Perth and I'm waiting for him at the finishing line. (There won't be a finishing line in reality, of course: it's his own private race. But this is the way it is in my dream.) He has his head down, and he's pushing his pedals harder than he's ever pushed them before.

I jump up and down, cheering him on; but he doesn't look up. He crosses the line, and he has this big, huge smile on his face; but *he doesn't look up*—

I wake up, panicking. *It's only a dream,* I tell myself. *A dream.* It's just been so long since I've seen him.

Then I remember what happened yesterday. I remember the exam, and I remember Lise, and I remember the argument I had with my mother. Anger swells up inside me again. *Hell,* I am so angry with my mother.

In the morning, I think about calling Sofe. But then I remember that she has an exam this morning; in fact, she'd be in there right now, scribbling away. I probably won't get to see her again properly until the exams are over: we don't study many of the same subjects. As for Mum's advice—to call Lise and talk to her—there's no way I'm following that. She's wrong, Mum. Talking doesn't help. It doesn't help Lise, anyway.

All morning, I try to study for my own next exam, which is in two days' time. (I mean, that's what exam week's about, isn't it? Cramming in, before each exam, all that work you should've done during the year?) I put my books on my desk, then spread them out on the floor, then pile them up on my desk again. Nothing works, though. I just keep thinking of Josh.

He'd understand, I think. He'd understand how I feel: about Lise *and* about Mum. He knows me. He does: he just *knows* me.

In the end, a couple of hours after midday, I pack up my books, leave a note on the kitchen table: *Caught the tram to Glenelg. Back for dinner.* The exams can wait. I *have* to see him; I have to *talk* to him. It's been too long.

Outside, it's hot: waves of heat splash against my skin as I traipse down to the tram stop. In the tram, my flesh sticks to the red vinyl seat through my clothes. My thoughts are dazzled, heat-drenched: I think of Josh, and of Mum, and of Lise, and of the exams to come. Then I give up and just think about Josh. Right now—right at this moment—he's all that matters to me. All I can think is, If I can just see him, things will be all right.

But when I arrive at the café, its door is locked and the "Closed" sign is up in the window. I peer through the glass: the lights are all off and the chairs are stacked on the tables. An early finish for Josh, then, because of the heat. He's probably at home right now, listening to one of his yodeling albums, lying on the floor with his shirt off and his feet up on the wall. (I can hear him saying, in that sexy, teasing voice of his, "It's cooler on the floor, Nat. Didn't you know? Heat rises.")

Hot waves of longing rush over me. I stand there on the pavement, hesitating. Josh's house is five minutes away, if you stick to the street instead of going via the beach. But we always used to walk the long way home together, via the beach, after work. Suddenly I want to prolong this moment on Jetty Road, prolong the pleasure of thinking about him, getting excited about seeing him again.

I head down toward the beach. At the roundabout, I cross over the tram tracks to the brick-paved plaza just in front of the beach. I walk slowly across it, past families eating ice cream at the green picnic tables. Seagulls circle and swoop in front of me, scavenging for leftover chips and discarded hamburgers. Ignoring them, I drift on, dreaming of Josh, past the last table and out onto the beachfront lawns.

A couple of women in their twenties are sitting at a table on the terrace outside the hotel; they glance up at me as I head toward the jetty. They're sipping at colorful drinks in tall, ice-filled glasses, gossiping. One of them rests her elbow on the table, leans over, says something, and the other one laughs—a long, languid, summer-lazy laugh. I think again, sharply, of Lise: of the times we came here, the secrets we told each other. (What about the secrets she told *Mum*?) Hastily, I look away from the women, back out to the beach.

It's then that I see him. He's sitting on the brick wall that borders the sea, not fifty yards in front of me. He has his back to me, but I'd know that tall, slight, broad-shouldered back anywhere. At the sight of him, I feel the old, familiar flurry of wings in my stomach.

It's Josh, and he is not alone.

The girl beside him on the brick wall is small and wiry, with dark, curly hair. They're sitting *very* close to each other. So close, in fact, that his hand is on her thigh. As I stand there, taking this in—trying to think, trying *not* to think—he leans into her and they kiss.

Deeply.

On the mouth.

All thoughts of Lise flee from my mind. For one long, sickening moment, I stand and watch them. My mind tumbles, stumbles on the truth. *Julie.* I know instantly that it's her.

Then, slowly, I turn around and trudge back toward the tram stop. I don't run; I don't hurry; I don't look back. I notice, surprised, how heavy my feet have become, dragging on the hot afternoon pavement. My stomach lurches and rolls. In my head, there is only one word: *Josh.* That's all I can think. *Josh.*

Back at the roundabout, while I wait for a gap in the cars, the world suddenly heaves. I bend over and throw up, onto the street. It feels like my whole *soul* is being wrenched out of me. Afterward, I straighten up, cross the road. I wait quietly at the tram stop, then sit with my head smearing the window on the way home. I can still taste the vomit in my mouth; I can smell it on my breath.

Josh—

chapter twenty-eight

One good reason

I throw up again several times when I get home. The third time, Dad comes into the bathroom, looking sympathetic.

"What's the matter, Nat? Did you eat something bad?"

He's like that, Dad: he's good with sick people. When I was a kid, it was always him, not Mum, who'd come into my bedroom if I had a temperature. He'd put a damp cloth on my forehead, offer to read me stories. He had such a comforting voice.

Now I shake my head in answer to his question, wipe my mouth with a piece of toilet paper. I don't think I've ever been sick so much in my *life.*

"Josh broke up with me today."

It's the closest I can get to saying the truth out loud. After I've told him, I turn away and walk into my bedroom. I close the door and lie down on my bed, staring up at the ceiling. I want to cry, but I can't. I feel too sick to cry.

My eyes close almost immediately, and I sleep. It's a long and deep sleep, and totally, *totally* dreamless.

In the morning, when I wake, the queasiness has passed and my stomach has settled. I lie in bed, listening to the familiar sounds of the house: the roof creaking, a floorboard shifting in the hall outside my room, the kitchen tap dripping.

When I get up, I find a note pinned up for me on the fridge. It's in Mum's handwriting:

Nat—

If you're still not well today, go to the doctor, okay? I've left the medical card and some money for you on my bedside table.

Love, Mum xxx

P.S. Dad says try some of his ginger tablets. They're good for the stomach.

I stand by the fridge in my pajamas, at a loss for words. If I hadn't argued with her the other day, I wouldn't have felt like I missed Josh so much, you know? And if I hadn't missed him so much, I wouldn't have gone to see him yesterday. Which would mean, I think now, irrationally, I wouldn't have seen what I saw.

I don't bother with a note back to her, and I leave the tablets on the kitchen table, untouched.

I'm going back to Jetty Road again. I've *got* to see him. Again.

* * *

Some days you can hear the sound of the ocean from Jetty Road, even as far back as the café. Today is one of those days, hot and still, the sky a deep, pulsating blue.

I march down the street toward the café, ignoring the sea and the sky. I head through the open door of the café. The place looks deserted—it's too early for customers—but I can hear someone moving about in the kitchen. A plate clatters, and the fridge door groans open. Then I hear the sound of someone humming. Yes, *humming.*

I go straight behind the counter, without calling out.

Josh is in the kitchen: he's standing at the stove, his back to me. At the sight of him, I feel my knees crumble. How could he? How *could* he? I take a deep breath, steeling myself.

"Where's Michael?" I demand, without bothering to say hello.

He swings around at my voice, startled. "Nat! I didn't hear you come in." His expression is unreadable. "Um—he's gone to the bank. Aren't you supposed to be at an exam or something?"

"My next one's tomorrow," I say.

He looks confused.

"I thought you weren't coming back till they were over."

"I *wasn't,*" I say grimly. "I need to talk to you, Josh."

A shadow crosses his face, and if there'd been a part of me that didn't believe what I saw yesterday—and there was, there *was;* how *could* it be true?—instantly it's gone.

"Now?" he says quietly.

"Now."

He doesn't protest. He can see it in my face already, I think; he knows I know.

He follows me out through the kitchen door, into the tiny backyard. I plunk myself down on the cement doorstep. Reluctantly, he sits down next to me. The yard is so small that there's only enough space, between us and the tin fence, for a couple of broken, discarded chairs from the café and the rusting refuse bin in the corner. His knee is squashed against my thigh, and there's no room to move away.

For a moment I can't bring myself to speak.

"I saw you and Julie."

He's silent. I plunge on.

"It *was* Julie, wasn't it? Yesterday. On the beach with you. Kissing."

Still he doesn't answer.

"Well? *Was* it?"

"Yes."

I sit there next to him on the step, wordless, staring at the refuse bin. Its lid is propped open, and bags of rubbish from the café spill out of it. A sudden memory slides into my mind: Josh and me, doing the last of the cleaning in the kitchen one afternoon; late winter, darkness already fallen. I'd switched off the CD player, and in the quietness that followed, we heard cats foraging around in the bin outside the kitchen. They hissed and spat at each other, fighting over leftover food or lost territory. Josh came up to me, put his arms around my shoulders. "Cats fighting," he murmured into my ear. "The strangest, loneliest sound in the world." He was right. It *is* a lonely sound.

I have so *many* memories like that of him in this place—

Next to me, Josh shifts uncomfortably on the step. His closeness—the feeling of his leg against mine—is almost unbearable.

"How long?" I say at last. "How long have you and Julie—?"

"A couple of weeks."

"Have you *slept* with her?"

"Yes," he says quietly.

There is a pause.

"It was only once, Nat. It was only—it was just last night." He hesitates, then says quickly, "I didn't want you to find out like this. I just saw so little of you over the last few weeks. You had your exams. And I was training with Julie every day. It just *happened*."

I squeeze myself against the wall, away from him.

"Screwing around doesn't just *happen,*" I say bitterly. "You *make* it happen."

Then my breath snags on something in my throat. *Screwing around*. They're not even my words; they're his. *You don't screw around when you're in a relationship, Nat. You just DON'T . . .*

I take another breath, suddenly shaky.

"I suppose you think *we* just happened—"

His silence hurts more than any words. I hear my breathing filling it, ragged with the first blinding tears.

"We can still be good friends," he says finally. His voice is soft, calm, appeasing as he trots out this last cliché. "Nat?"

But I am too choked to answer. We both listen—equally astonished, I think—to the strange, noisy, abandoned sobs coming out of me. After a moment, he sighs and stands up, having to press against me even to do this. He glances down at me, then pushes open the kitchen door and walks back into the café.

I don't move. For a long, long time I don't move. The sweet-sour stench of refuse drifts over to me from the bin, and there is plenty of room for me, here on the step, now that I am alone. Far off in the background, I hear the sound of the sea.

It's a lonely, lonely sound, the sea. When I think about it now, I think *that's* the loneliest sound in the world.

Michael's voice over the phone later that day is unimpressed.

"It's nearly Christmas, Nat. This is the busiest time of the year."

It's not like I even liked the job, I think bitterly.

"I've just sacked Loretta," he goes on. "*Finally.* We really *need* you here. Give me one good reason why you have to quit your job now."

One good reason? That's easy. He's long and lean and dark-eyed, and he's probably standing at Michael's elbow in his black-and-white checked pants right now.

My breath catches. I try not to let my voice wobble.

"I'm sorry, Michael. This is a temporary job. I don't have to give you a reason at all."

I mean, what else can I do? I can't work with Josh anymore. I can't stand near to him, smell him, look into his eyes. I just *can't.*

I put the phone down, go back to my desk, open my books. That's all there is left to do.

chapter twenty-nine

Everything

The next couple of weeks are a blur.

At home, I study for my remaining exams. When I'm not studying, I eat chocolate, watch TV, sleep, eat more chocolate. I don't know why I eat so much chocolate, except that it's sweet, smooth, soothing. It slows my tears.

Mum comes into the living room sometimes to interrupt my TV stupor. She sits down next to me on the sofa, offers her standard fare: talk, sympathy, understanding. When she does this, I push her away. I don't *want* understanding right now, especially not hers; I haven't forgotten that argument we had about Lise the other day. Despite everything else that's happened to me since, I haven't forgotten.

One morning, though, when my parents and Tim are out at work, I call Sofe. I have this sudden urge to hear her voice—her brash, cheerful voice. Maybe *she* can make me feel better.

I speak flatly as I tell her what's happened, trying not to cry.

"What an asshole," she says angrily before I can even finish. "You are *so* well rid of him—"

Immediately I feel the tears gathering again. Her anger doesn't help; it makes me feel worse. I say goodbye hastily and hang up. Maybe only chocolate *can* make me feel better, after all.

In between chocolate sessions, I put on my uniform, go to school, and take my exams. Once—only once—I see Lise there. She doesn't come to any of the exams, but one day, as I'm crossing the schoolyard, I catch sight of her standing outside the library. She's dressed in regular clothes, looking scrawny and wispy, as if the hot north wind could blow her away, and she's deep in conversation with Jessica Fuller, whose hand is on her shoulder. Somehow, inevitably, I am reminded of Mum. *Talking,* I think briefly, with scorn—*what good does THAT do? That's what SHE did with Lise.*

But the thought passes. I don't go over to Lise and Jessica; I don't wave; I walk straight into the exam room and don't turn back. I know that I should, but I don't. The truth is, I can't think about Lise right now: her life, her future. There is no lasting room for anyone else inside this blankness of mine: I am consumed with the process of keeping myself alive, afloat.

I wanted everything with Josh, you know? Not just to be friends. *Everything.*

At night I lie in my bed in the dark, touching the places where he touched me. My skin feels cold without the warmth of his against it. I long for the brush of his lips across mine, the fresh, musty smell of his armpits after a bike ride, the warm tickle of his breath against my face. It feels like I've crash-landed onto a planet where I don't belong. There is no map here, and the only person who could give me direction in this place—show me north, south, east, west, all the nooks and crannies in between—will never come.

I close my eyes at last and slide into sleep. His face—laughing brown eyes, freckles across the nose, straight blond hair—lies just beneath my eyelids. It's the weirdest thing: he's so close to me like this. Closer than he's ever been, and so far out of reach.

chapter thirty

Sleep

The day before my last exam, Mum comes into the living room. Ignoring my hostile glare, she goes over to the TV, switches it off.

"Can I talk to you for a moment, sweetie?"

I sigh. "You've turned off the TV, haven't you? I don't have much choice."

She decides to ignore this, too.

"I've got some good news about Lise."

So this is it, I think, dragging myself unwillingly out of my thoughts about Josh: Lise, the topic I've been avoiding talking about with her for so long. Has she even noticed how quiet I've been around her? How much I've been *avoiding* her?

Mum perches on the corner of the coffee table in front of my armchair.

"I'm not supposed to tell you this, of course, but I know you've been worried." She gives me a quick, hopeful look. "Lise rang me this morning. She wanted the name of a counselor."

She smiles at me. It's a gentle, satisfied, *smug* little smile.

"I just thought you'd like to know," she says.

I stare at her in disbelief.

"That's *it*? *That's* your good news?"

She nods, her smile wavering. Anger fills me all over again—like it did with her the other day—only this time I am ready for it.

I look her straight in the eye. "What help's a counselor going to be for Lise?"

She opens her mouth.

"All counselors do is *talk,*" I say scornfully, before she can speak. "*You're* a counselor. What help were *you* to Lise that day she came over to talk to you? She didn't even make it through the exams."

Mum swallows.

"That's a bit harsh, Nat."

Not HARSH, I think, looking away, not speaking. *Accurate, maybe. Fair.*

"I think there's something you should know," Mum says finally.

I shrug. *Tell me if you want to. See if I care.*

"That day Lise came over," she says quietly. "You said the other day I should've done something. But the thing is, I *did.*" She pauses. "A couple of days after her visit, I called her mother."

She stops, waiting for me to say something. When I don't, she sighs and goes on.

"I tried to talk to Jen about Lise. I told her I thought Lise needed treatment."

"And?" I say, despite myself.

Mum rubs her eyes wearily. "She said she had it 'covered.'"

When I still don't speak, she lifts her hands, palms up, to the ceiling. "There was nothing more I could do, Nat. Lise is Jen's daughter, not mine."

Rage fills me again, only this time I don't know who it's directed at. Mrs. Mawson? Mum? Lise? Josh? *Myself*? I say the first thing that comes into my head.

"Yeah, *well*. That's the first time *I'd* ever noticed."

Mum looks down at her hands in her lap. When she lifts her head again, I can see the hurt in her eyes.

I don't say anything. I get up, go over to the TV, switch it back on. Then I sit down again and stare at it pointedly. It's less than a minute before Mum, too, gets up. She leaves the room without speaking, closing the door quietly behind her.

As soon as she's gone, my eyes fill with tears. Here I am, alone in this room yet again. Why did I *do* that? Why did I argue with her about Lise? Haven't we said it all before? After what she's just told me about Mrs. Mawson, I don't even know if I'm angry about it anymore.

The truth is, I'm just tired—so, *so* tired. Of everything: of studying for exams, worrying about Lise, arguing with Mum. I don't have the energy for it anymore: I've used it all up on Josh. All I can think right now is, *What about me? Why doesn't Mum ask about ME?*

I get up, steal out of the living room, down the corridor to my bedroom. I crawl into my bed, turn to face the wall, shut my eyes. Then I sleep.

Sweet, sweet sleep: I feel like I could sleep forever.

chapter thirty-one

Sausages

My parents throw a celebration barbecue for dinner after my last exam. Tim and his girlfriend, Sally, join us at the last moment. Dad picks tomatoes and parsley from his veggie garden and makes a salad, muttering about the spring onions that died on the last 100-degree scorcher a couple of days ago: "They'd have tasted so good with these tomatoes." Then we sit around the outdoor table on the porch, facing the brown, scraggly, bare-patched lawn. Mosquitoes whine at our ears.

While Mum's back in the kitchen pouring herself a second glass of wine, the phone rings. She picks it up, murmurs into it, calls out: "It's for you, Nat."

My insides flutter with stupid, inevitable hope. I stumble toward the screen door, take the phone from her.

"Nat?"

It's Lise. I sink back to earth.

"Am I interrupting anything?"

I can smell the sausages smoking on the barbecue. (Why don't vegetarian patties smell like that?) Suddenly I realize how *long* it is since I've spoken to Lise.

"No, no," I say hastily. "Go for it."

She hesitates. Then she says simply, "I was just ringing to tell you I'm going into the hospital soon. They've just put me on the waiting list."

My mind reels. "The hospital?" I echo.

Lise takes a breath. "I've been seeing this counselor—well, this psychiatrist, actually—and I've realized—I don't know—" She stops, then starts again. "I've just *got* to start eating."

How hard can it be to eat? I wonder.

"It's harder than it sounds, Nat," she says, like she's reading my mind.

The words hang between us over the phone. I try to tease some kind of sense out of them.

"This program I'm going into, in the hospital," she says at last. "It's specially designed for people with anorexia. To give them support while they put on weight."

There. Finally, after all this time, the moment of truth. *My friend Lise, the anorexic.*

"Are you scared?" I ask her slowly.

"No," she says, sounding puzzled. "I thought I would be, but I'm not. It's what I need."

That's when I notice something different in her voice, something I haven't heard for a long time, if ever. At first I can't put my finger on it. Then I realize that it sounds like—*hope*?

"Things've changed," she says slowly, as if the words that she's saying are unfamiliar to her, like a new language. "I *want* to get better. I really do."

My eyes well up at her words, like so many times recently. But they're not tears of self-pity this time: they're tears of pure, simple shame. All this time, I've been thinking of my own problems, and here Lise is, going through stuff I can't even begin to imagine.

"Lise?" I say, humbly.

"Yeah?"

"Can I come and visit you? In the hospital, I mean."

"Do you want to?" she asks, surprised.

"Of course I do," I say, wiping another tear away. "You're my *friend*."

From the garden, the clink of glasses drifts up to me, mingled with the cheerful voices of my parents laughing with Tim and Sally. Suddenly I can't face all that blatant happiness. I can't help myself: I just have to be alone.

In my bedroom, I lie curled up on the bed, cocooned. I glance at the letter on my desk which I started to write to Josh earlier this afternoon: I got halfway and then couldn't bear the sound of my own whining, even on paper, and stopped. Next to it is a picture of Sofe and Lise and me, taken at the Year 11 school camp: we're standing on the beach in our bathing suits, arms across each other's shoulders, hair dripping. Sofia has her mouth open in a wide, white-toothed smile, and Lise is laughing, her curly wet hair draping the smooth, generous curves of her body.

I roll onto my other side, facing the door, and tuck my head into my elbow. Everything used to be so simple before, so *right,* I think, wiping away yet another tear: Lise eating ice cream on a cold winter's day; Josh cuddling up to me, murmuring sweet things in my ear. What *happened*?

There's a knock on my door. Mum pokes her head around, sees me on the bed.

"Oh, sweetie," she says, her eyes crinkling up with sympathy.

She comes into the room, sits beside me on the bed.

"Lise is going into the hospital," I say desolately.

She nods. "It's the best place for her now, isn't it?"

We look at each other for a moment without speaking. Something passes between us then—some tacit kind of understanding, something that loosens the knot that's been inside of me recently whenever I'm around her. The time for anger between us is over, I realize. At least for now.

I want to apologize to her, to say: *I know you did everything you could for Lise.* Because I can see now that she did, you know? She *did.* That's what she was trying to tell me the other day, in front of the TV. But I can't bring myself to say the words aloud. Mum and I—we're not good at that sort of stuff. Despite all her "social working" on me, I still can't bring myself to say the things she wants me to say, the things I *should* say. I just can't. Because the thing is, then where would I be? Would there be any me at all?

So instead we just have this moment together—this moment of unspoken, tenuous peace.

"I wasn't a very good friend to Lise this year," I say finally.

"We all did our best, Nat," she says, ever the positive thinker, ever the social worker. "You, too."

Did I, though? I wonder. The truth is, sometimes I think that Sofe was a better friend to Lise this year than me. At least she was *honest* with her. At least she had the guts to speak out.

Mum sits silently with me for a couple more moments. Then she picks up another photo—the one on my bedside table. It's Josh and me at the Formal—that wide, idiotic, *happy* grin of mine.

"Do you miss him, Nat?" she asks quietly.

I don't say anything. My throat clots with tears that I try desperately to hold back. She strokes my hair, and her touch sets me off yet again. I didn't know it was *possible* to cry so much.

"I miss him every moment of the day, Mum," I say through my tears.

"I know."

"I can't imagine life without him. It doesn't make sense."

Some time later, after I've cried a whole *sea* of tears, I sit up and grab a tissue from the bedside table. Mum smiles at me, puts her hands on each of my shoulders, holding me at arm's length. I can smell the white wine on her breath, that familiar, tipsy-summer-evening smell of hers. She gazes into my eyes, says simply, "Time, Nat." She nods firmly, without looking away. "That's what it takes. *Time.*"

Then, for a while, we sit there, side by side on the bed. We don't talk. There's just the smell of barbecue smoke drifting in through the window and the hum of a stray mosquito homing in on its target. The feel of my mother beside me, solid, dependable, *there.* That's all. Just *there.*

Afterward, we go back out to the garden together. I am red-eyed and shaky, but finally calm.

Dad grins at me, deliberately oblivious of my tear-streaked face. "Have a sausage, Nat. It's December. There's still time to break your New Year's resolution."

I look at the sausage he's holding out to me and think of Lise, whose suggestion it was, all those months ago, to go vegetarian together. I think of all she gave up when she started down that track, and where it got her. Then I think of Josh: the way he used to come up behind me in the kitchen at the Wild Carrot, put his arms around my waist, croon "Broccoli, broccoli" at me. Loretta never did understand why I laughed so much while I was washing the dishes.

I am *so* sick of feeling crappy, you know?

"Okay," I hear myself saying loudly. "*Yes.* I'll have one."

He hands the sausage to me, folded up in bread. I hold it in my hands; it's warm and sloppy with tomato sauce, the butter on the bread stained black by the grill. I feel momentarily like I'm a kid again—those endless summer barbecues, the welcome pleasure of respite from Mum's lousy cooking.

I can feel them all watching me anxiously as I take my first bite; I think they half expect me to spit it back out at them, go running around the back lawn shrieking wild things about animals and slaughterhouses.

But I don't. There's a limit, I think, to feeling sorry for yourself. There's only so much misery you can allow yourself before some little stubborn part of you bounces back in rebellion.

"It's *delicious,*" I tell them with a tentative grin. I eat the rest of it, then say, "Are there any more sausages left?"

Dad hands me a second one, wordlessly. I bite into it, and for a moment, at least, the world is sunny and still and free of grief.

chapter thirty-two

Under the peppercorn trees

Several weeks later, there's only one more torture left for the school to inflict on us: Speech Day. Even though, as Year 12s, we haven't been back to school since our exams ended, we're still expected to turn up on the last day of term, dressed in the regulation knee-length socks, school ties, and blazers, prayer books in hand. It's like some kind of final sadistic punishment designed to make you really hope you've passed.

Sofia and I both arrive unexpectedly early. We linger around under the scanty shade of the peppercorn trees down by the tennis courts, chatting, and she gives me the latest update on her going-around-Australia saga.

"Nick finally got the VW going."

"Really? So when're you going?"

"Sunday."

I blink. "*Sunday?* As in *this* Sunday?"

She nods, breaking out into an excited grin. "First stop,

Great Ocean Road." Then, seeing the expression on my face, she laughs. "C'mon, Nat. It's not like I'm going forever."

She's right, of course. I know Sofe: she'll be back, in her own good time. It's just, I wasn't expecting her to leave so soon.

"Promise you'll send some postcards," I say plaintively.

"Of course. *Stacks.*"

"To Lise, too?"

She sighs. "To Lise, too."

I gaze at the chain-link fence, the tennis court a green blur behind it. *Will* she write to Lise? Somehow I can't imagine it. What would Sofia say on a postcard to Lise, anyway?

Aloud, I say, "You'll have to send everything care of the hospital. She gets admitted tomorrow."

Sofia sighs again, this time with palpable impatience. "Hospital, schmospital," she says. "I'm just not *into* this whole starving thing."

I stare at her incredulously. I mean, surely a little concern wouldn't go astray here?

"It's a waste of time, Nat—that's what gets me," she says, tugging moodily at a peppercorn branch swaying over her head. "Playing skinny, playing frail. Playing the loser."

"Yeah, but—"

She plucks a peppercorn frond off the tree and brushes it across her face, her nose ring winking defiantly in the dappled sunlight.

"I think she should just *get a life.*"

I look up through the trees to the deep blue sky above us, saying nothing. If only it was as easy as that.

"She hasn't just got anorexia, you know," I say quietly. "There's other stuff going on with her, too."

"Like what?" asks Sofia, puzzled.

So I repeat what Lise told me on the phone a couple of nights ago when she called again: about the fear that crawls up her throat during the day, the nausea that keeps her awake at night. Apparently, she had no idea what these things were until she described them to one of the hospital doctors during a preadmission assessment the other day. "Panic attacks," he called them.

Sofe groans. "Why didn't she tell anyone?"

I shrug. "Who knows? Maybe she thought it would go away."

But in my head, I can still hear what Lise said when I asked her the same thing over the phone.

"I couldn't tell anyone," she said, in a voice that rang with loneliness. "I thought I was going *mad*—"

Next to me on the bench, Sofe yawns, no doubt already warming up for the speeches we're about to be subjected to in the assembly hall. Her yawn makes me smile wryly, and she grins back at me, but neither of us says anything for a while. We sit on the bench in peaceful companionship, and I let my thoughts drift. I find myself thinking back over the year, and for a sudden, poignant moment, I am flooded with images: Josh in his suit at the Year 12 Formal; the chocolate cake I made so hopefully for Lise; Sofe unrepentantly brandishing her nose ring the day she got suspended.

Then, for some reason, my thoughts wander even further back, to that day in the living room when Lise talked to

Sofia and me about New Year's resolutions. The image is still so clear in my mind that I can see the ceiling fans rotating above our heads, feel the sweat collecting on my upper lip, hear the bright, optimistic, determined way she said, "Let's go vegetarian. It's *good* for you."

Sometimes I think that day in the living room was like the starting point. Of *everything,* you know? Of Lise becoming anorexic; of me getting the job at the Wild Carrot Café; of Sofe going out with the first guy she's ever felt serious about in her life. After we made that resolution, everything changed.

A sudden thought occurs to me. I turn to Sofia.

"Remember our New Year's resolution?"

She nods.

"I've got something to confess," I tell her sheepishly. "I didn't stick to it." Then I add hastily, "But Lise didn't, either."

An expression of mock horror passes across her face.

"*Lise* didn't stick to a *resolution*?"

I shake my head. "The dietitian at the hospital says she has to eat meat while she's there."

Sophia rolls her eyes. "What—anorexics aren't allowed to be vegetarian? They're not allowed to have a conscience?"

I shrug. "Something like that. Anyway, what about *you*? Did you keep your New Year's resolution?"

"Mate," she says simply, "I can't *imagine* eating meat now. I'm even buying cruelty-free soaps and shampoos."

I almost laugh out loud. I mean, sticking to things has never exactly been Sofe's strong point.

But when she sees my face, she frowns.

"No, for *real.* Did you know that jellybeans are made with calves' feet? The gelatin in them, I mean. And guess what? Cheese has rennet in it, and that's made from the lining of a cow's stomach."

That's when I realize she's serious.

She's changed, Sofia. It's weird, you know? In some ways, I think I've always seen her as unchangeable. *Different,* yes, with her cigarettes, her colorful clothes, her mum's backyard dope plant—but still, somehow, constant. Now, though, it comes to me suddenly that her life has changed as much in the last year as mine—as much, even, as Lise's. Meeting Nick has made her, not happier, exactly (she's *always* been happy), but calmer. More settled. It's like she's found a life that's *right* for her.

But now that I think about this, am I surprised? About the vegetarian bit, maybe; but the rest of it—no. Not really.

Somehow I always knew Sofe would find her own path.

chapter thirty-three

Song

Later, in the school hall, I shift uncomfortably in my chair. Up on stage, the speeches and endless prize-giving ceremonies drag on. (When I say endless, I mean *endless.* There's even a prize for Christian Student Leader of the Year.) Every now and then, the monotony is broken by the headmistress requesting a prayer, and the whole hall rustles as we all kneel down and say the prayer before scrambling back up to our seats again.

On my left, in between prayers, Sofe doodles with a chewed-up pen in the margins of her hymnbook. Lise sits to my right, pale and serious in a uniform that seems to engulf her, swallow her whole. Every time she bends her head, the little vertebra at the top of her spine pops out like a sharp pebble. She looks ready—*so* ready—for the hospital. It's not that she's skeletal, exactly. But you can't help seeing that she's on the way. *Well* on the way.

I sigh and move restlessly again on my seat. On the piano

at the front of the hall, Lucy Nguyen, the school's Year 11 musical genius, starts playing the introduction to the school hymn. As we stand up obediently, I think suddenly of Josh. He would have laughed at Speech Day: at the hymns and the prayers; at all these little school rituals we go through. He'd have been right, too: they *are* stupid. But the thing is, he never *did* see this part—the school part—of my life.

Now, of course, it's the whole *rest of my life* that he'll never know.

It's not the first time I've thought of Josh today: every day, he darts in and out of my thoughts like this, pricking me with memories, making me ache. Sometimes, when I'm with Sofe, she picks up on it. She digs me in the waist, says, "You've got the thinking-of-the-asshole look on your face again."

That's what I like about Sofe. She brings you back to earth.

Now I glance at Lise to distract myself. She's standing rock-still, her small wrist frail under the weight of the hymn-book. Nothing about her—*nothing*—is relaxed. Her body strains forward, yearning toward the piano at the front of the hall, and her mouth is a thin, tense line, jaw muscles taut, clenching. It's like she's afraid to sing, afraid to open her mouth in case nothing comes out. Like she's afraid she's lost her *voice.*

I feel a sudden hard lump in my throat. I know how she feels, I think. I feel like I've lost my voice, too, you know? Had it stolen away from me, just when I was at my strongest and happiest. It's like I lost all my songs when Josh left, and now I can't imagine ever finding any new ones.

But then the introduction to the hymn finishes, and it's time for us to start singing. As always—unlike the rest of us, who are all way too cool to open our mouths during hymns—Lise sings. Now that she's singing, the tension in her body has gone: she sings with a wide-open, honest mouth; she sings strong and true. Standing next to her, listening to her sing someone else's words, I find myself wondering if I'll ever get the chance to hear her real voice, the real Lise; *her* song, *her* words. Somehow, I always missed it before; somehow, I never heard it.

The hymn ends. As we sit down, Lise turns to me. She catches my glance, holds it. Then, slowly, tremulously, she smiles. It's a sweet, wide smile in that achingly hungry face—a smile that's full of promise.

Life is good. That's what that smile whispers.

epilogue

Nat

Lise's room in the Psych Ward is gray. The view through the venetian blinds over the window is gray: cloudy late-summer skies above, gray concrete car park below. Inside the room, the colors are no different—gray-painted walls, plastic gray visitors' chairs, spotted gray linoleum floors that smell of nurses' rubber soles and bleach. Practically the only oasis of color in the whole place is the quilt that Lise brought with her: it's yellow, with seashells and starfish and sea horses.

"To remind me of the beach," she told me the first day I visited. "And of the *good* times."

It reminds me of the beach, too: of walking up and down Jetty Road under the sea-blue sky; of the smell of salt in the air, and the taste of ice cream, and the promise of good things to come.

It reminds me, too, of that conversation Lise and I had at the start of the year in the Italian coffee shop, after we'd applied for the job at the Wild Carrot. *I'd like to change everything about myself,* she told me. *I'd like to be someone else completely.*

Seeing Lise here in the hospital, week after week, I've started to think: Is that what it's all about, this anorexia nervosa? About hating yourself so much you despise the way you look, the way you feel? The way you *are*?

If so—if that's how it really feels, I mean—I can imagine how you might want to escape yourself. I can imagine how you might try to just whittle yourself away. You might even just want to keep on whittling, until there was nothing of you left at all.

The other colorful thing in Lise's room is the postcard pinned up on the wall above her bed. It's a picture of somewhere on the Great Ocean Road: sparkling seas, steep cliffs, crumbling rocks. Lise waved it in front of me one day a couple of weeks into her stay in the hospital, and then showed me the message on the back:

Dear Lise,
How's things. We're having a ball. Nick says hi. Eat a few Tim Tams for me.
Love as always, Sofe.

I've thought about the message on that card a lot since then, about what it means. I was wrong about Sofe and Lise, you know: they *do* care about each other, underneath. I shouldn't have been so scared of their arguments: of the things they might say to each other one day, of the things that could never get taken back. I should have known they'd work things out, in their own way. Not that they'll ever be close or anything, but—they understand where they are with each other these days, and it's okay. Maybe it always was.

I was wrong about something else, too—the Year 12 results. Not about Sofe, of course, who got into nursing as planned: she sent in her notice of deferment from somewhere on the Central Coast, hopped back into the VW and probably hasn't thought about it since. Me, though—I got into uni. Can you believe that? The wonders of cramming, hey. Now all I have to do is figure out what I'm going to *study* there.

But it was Lise's results that I was most wrong about: she failed. I mean, I know she only took half an exam in the end—but I guess I kind of assumed that her marks during the year would make up for that, or that she'd be given some kind of medical exemption.

"My marks during the year were crap," she tells me one day in the hospital, when I finally get up the courage to ask her what happened. "I kept having panic attacks during tests and assignments and stuff." She takes a deep breath and then adds, "And I don't want to apply for an exemption."

I stare at her incredulously. "Why not?"

She shrugs. "It was a bad year, Nat. I want to put it behind me."

For a moment, neither of us says anything. I look at her now, as she stares out the window. She's put on weight: she's up to 105 pounds now, and only has 15 more to go to reach her "target weight." She's still pretty slender, though—and despite all the ready-made optimism and antidepressants the hospital has pumped into her, there's this kind of fragile, wounded look in her eyes. Like she's afraid to offer herself up to the world, in case she gets hurt again.

Not for the first time, I find myself wondering how she'll cope when she leaves the hospital. I mean, I know she'll still be having appointments with the dietitian, going to see her psychiatrist, coming up to the hospital a couple of times a week for a meal. But she's the one who has to put the food in her mouth; she's the one who's got to give herself a chance. I don't know whether she can do it, to be honest; it scares me even thinking about it.

"So what're you going to do this year?" I ask cautiously. "Repeat Year 12?"

She shakes her head. "I'm having a year off."

"Really?" I say, surprised. "To do—what?"

She hesitates. "Get a job?"

"What about your parents? What do *they* say?"

She doesn't answer straightaway. I look at her carefully. Sometimes, coming in here to visit her, I've run into one or another member of her family. Terri always stops to chat with me, ask me how things are going: she seems sad about what's happened with Lise but still cheerful in herself, if that makes any sense. ("She plays lots of card games with me," Lise told me once. "And she brings in lots of soppy girly videos for us to watch." She gave me a surprised grin then. "It's been really *good,* actually.")

Lise's father, too, always maintains a cheery smile when he sees me: "Not much longer now, Nat. She'll be out of here soon." But Mrs. Mawson never looks anything but distressed. Sometimes she looks sad-distressed; sometimes she looks confused-distressed; sometimes she just looks plain *furious*-distressed. I can only imagine what family therapy sessions must be like with her. (Family therapy is one of the parts of Lise's treatment.)

Now Lise says to me, "It doesn't matter what my parents say about what I want to do this year." A determined look has come across her face. "I've *got* to give myself some time, Nat. Studying can wait. I have to get my *life* together first."

Her voice is firm, her eyes steady on mine. There's not even a hint of the old staring-down-at-the-floor routine that used to be such a part of her. Maybe she *will* make it when she gets out of the hospital, I think, with sudden renewed respect. Maybe she'll make it with flying colors.

In fact, with that look of steely determination, maybe she's not so fragile after all. Maybe she's the strongest of the lot of us—

The day before Lise is discharged from the hospital, I tell her about my swimmer/drifter theory. I've never mentioned it to anyone else before.

She understands immediately what I mean, as I knew she would. "Sofe's a swimmer, right?"

I nod. "She's always heading off where she wants to, you

know? Even if she doesn't know exactly where she's heading *to.*"

We laugh.

"You're a swimmer, too," I add.

"Me?"

I nod again. "I've admired your iron will ever since I met you, you know? You're always going *somewhere*—even if it's the wrong way, sometimes." I grin at her ruefully. "You'll plow back to shore one of these days."

Because I believe this now. I really do.

Lise, meanwhile, is making other connections. "Josh was a swimmer, too, wasn't he?" she says softly.

I swallow. It's true, of course; I've always known that. That's probably why I fell for him so hard in the first place. Josh was so full of color and vitality and direction, it was easy to get lost in him, to feel like my life had started to reflect those qualities, too. Now that he's gone, I'm back to where I was before I met him—drifting, drifting. Floating aimlessly on a calm, calm sea.

"Nat?"

I come back to earth. "Mmm?"

"It's okay to talk about it if you want to, you know," Lise says gently. "I mean, maybe you talk to Sofe, or to your mum, or whatever—I don't know. But if not, I'm here, okay? I'm *here.*"

There's a sudden lump in my throat. "You're a good friend, you know that, Lise Mawson?" I say gruffly.

"So're you," she says, regarding me gravely.

Then suddenly—I don't know who reaches out first—we're hugging. Me and Lise, my un-huggy friend: arms around each other, holding on for dear life. It's weird, but at that moment, for the first time, I know things are going to be all right. *Really* all right, I mean. Like Sofe said on that postcard, in her typical, Sofia-like way: friendship is what matters. As long as you've got friends, you'll be okay.

My chin rests on Lise's shoulder as I hold her, and my eyes fall on the window. There are a million things you can see when you look out a window, I suppose—clouds, cars, bad weather, traffic lights, parking meters. But what I see is the sky.

That's the thing about drifting, I realize with a sudden, warm rush of gladness. Lying on your back, floating, that's exactly what you see: the whole inviting, wide-open sky.

Afterword

Anorexia nervosa affects up to one percent of adolescent girls and is the third-commonest ongoing health problem in females of this age. Eating disorders are much more common in females than males, about nine times more common in adolescence and three times more common in prepubertal children. Anorexia nervosa may occur from eight years of age, while bulimia nervosa commonly starts in late adolescence. Recovery often takes many years, the health complications affect every system in the body, and there is a risk of death.

Leaving Jetty Road uses the imaginative ploy of interweaving three friends' different paths through adolescence to highlight some common features in those who develop eating disorders and the insidious way in which these evolve. While the character and circumstances of girls who develop eating disorders are individual, some features are common, and Lise, in contrast to her friends, displays many of these.

She is intense, determined, shows self-control, and has high body dissatisfaction. She has trouble establishing age-appropriate relationships, has high anxiety, and is a perfectionist about her studies. Her family values body image, and her mother is very food conscious. Of course, not everyone who has these characteristics develops an eating disorder and not everyone with an eating disorder displays all of these characteristics. There is a strong genetic factor that puts some at risk, and eating disorders commonly run in families. Typically, Lise elects to become vegetarian, stops using butter, and develops rigid rules relating to food, such as fasting before exams and an aversion to wheat. When she does relax her rules, she exercises to compensate for the calories taken. She indulges in isolated exercise for weight control rather than team sports for pleasure. Initially she is rewarded with compliments for weight loss, but it is never enough; she strives for lower and lower weights. She is unable to see her weight loss as a disease, but rather sees it as an achievement. Parents can perpetuate these behaviors by buying diet foods, allowing extreme exercise, and buying clothes in small sizes.

So how do you determine when someone you know is not eating healthily and could be developing an eating disorder? Concern should be raised if eating or exercise behaviors become habitual, chronic, and intrude on that person's life. Healthy eaters eat because they are hungry or for enjoyment, at reasonable intervals; are flexible, not anxious about occasional sweet or fatty foods; can eat comfortably in company; and don't set their lives around food rules. Sadly, some young people who set out to prove their self-discipline by controlling their eating and exercise patterns get taken over by the eating disorder and become unable to stop the behaviors that tend to develop. Early treatment is associated with better outcomes, so recognizing the problem and seeking help early are important. However, often the person is likely to deny there is a problem, is not willing to relinquish the eating disorder, and will make false promises to avoid treatment. Getting the person to accept help is usually not easy, but it is the first step on a long road to recovery.

Patricia McVeagh
Medical Coordinator
Sydney Children's Hospital, Eating Disorder Unit

Acknowledgments

Writing this book would not have been possible without the assistance of a Varuna Award for Manuscript Development. It would have been equally impossible without the incredibly warm and enthusiastic support of Vanessa Radnidge, Lisa Berryman, and Sam Rich at HarperCollins in Australia. Thanks are also due to Kim Swivel, who did the final copyedit, and to my hardworking agent, Barbara Mobbs.

Further thanks go to my American editing and publishing team at Knopf Books for Young Readers, and in particular to Erin Clarke, for her hard work and warm, friendly transatlantic e-mails. One day maybe we'll meet in person, Erin!

Thank you, too, to my parents (for their incorrigible pride in me, and for being such amazing, inveterate, and underpaid publicists for *Leaving Jetty Road*), to my sister, Sarah (for her love, her unswervingly generous friendship, and—of course!—the Bollinger), and to all those enthusiastic, foolhardy friends of mine who agreed to read various drafts of this book along the way.

My final thanks go to my readers (adults and young adults alike), as well as to various bookshop owners, school librarians, and schoolteachers. The continuing level of their warmth and encouragement humbles me. I always knew that I would enjoy the writing process itself, but they have helped me to enjoy the aftermath of the writing process, and I can't say how grateful I am.